Life Without Alice

Both Brenda and Alice perked up when I walked in.

"What's new?" Alice asked me.

The blank look on my face must have answered the question, because Brenda's face fell and Alice began to blush. Brenda shot Alice a strange look and then lowered her eyes. All of a sudden, I got the message. I was embarrassing Alice. She was *ashamed* of me.

Who could blame her? According to Susannah, she'd been bragging about me all over Hope House. And now, instead of breezing in like a big wheel, I was plopping myself down like a big dud and expecting four sick kids to entertain me. I started blushing too. *I* was ashamed of me.

And that was the beginning of my career as a compulsive liar. I don't know what came over me. Once I got started, I couldn't stop. The kids were so impressed with me it was irresistible. And when I saw the look on Alice's face, it convinced me I was doing the right thing.

Also available in Lions

The Monster Garden *Vivien Alcock*
Split Second *Nick Baker*
My Teacher Fried My Brains *Bruce Coville*
Spellhorn *Berlie Doherty*
A Sound of Chariots *Mollie Hunter*
The Fib *George Layton*
The Summer Riders *Patricia Leitch*
Rabble Starkey *Lois Lowry*
The Lucky Stone *Jahnna Malcolm*
My Mate Shofiq *Jan Needle*
Something Really Wild *Colin Pearce*
Daredevils or Scaredycats *Chris Powling*
Shapeshifter *Laurence Staig*
Gemma *Noel Streatfeild*
Double Exposure *Andrew Taylor*
Death Knell *Nicholas Wilde*

Life without Alice

Jan Kenneth

Lions
An Imprint of HarperCollins*Publishers*

First published in the US
by HarperCollins Publishers Inc. 1993
First published in Great Britain in Lions 1993

Lions is an imprint of HarperCollins Children's Books,
a division of HarperCollins Publishers Ltd,
77/85 Fulham Palace Road,
Hammersmith, London W6 8JB

ISBN 0 00 674774–4

Set in Bembo
Printed and bound in Great Britain by
HarperCollins Manufacturing, Glasgow

1

Let me put it this way, my sister Alice could talk to a potted plant and have that potted plant talking back. Maybe even telling jokes and showing off. When you think Alice, think personality to the max and you get the idea.

I, on the other hand, am more the potted-plant type. I get tongue-tied round people I don't know — especially boys. A lot of the time I'd rather read and write in my diary than hang out with a group of kids. And I never know what it's cool to wear.

Actually, when we moved to Somerset, Indiana, just before the start of a new school year, Alice wasn't one hundred percent sure about that either. But she knew how to find out. "I'd say it's time for a little reconnaissance mission," she said with a grin.

Next thing I know, Alice is rigging us up a couple of "spy" outfits – dark sunglasses, baseball hats, and long raincoats with the belts cinched tight and the collars turned up.

Agent Alice and Agent Lily. Identical spies. Identical twins. We looked in the mirror and cracked up. Even in disguise we looked exactly alike.

"OK," she said, tucking her hair up under her cap. "Our objective at this point is strictly surveillance. Do not engage with the indigenous personnel. Simply observe. Do you understand? We don't want to make our debut in Somerset until we know exactly what to wear."

"Fully," I said, giving her a snappy salute.

"Good. Let's move out."

We were skulking towards the front door – (practising our spy moves, you understand) – when Mum came down the stairs and started laughing. She was carrying a box of kitchen stuff that the movers had left upstairs by mistake. "Where are you two going in that get-up?" she giggled.

"Sorry, Mum, we're not free to divulge that information at this time," Alice told her in her CIA operative voice.

"It's really better this way," I said, nodding

seriously. "The less you know, the safer you'll be."

Mum laughed again and didn't ask us any more questions. "OK. OK," she grinned. "As long as you two are together I'm not going to worry. I know you'll look out for each other."

She was right about that. Alice and I did look out for each other. We had to, since it was just Mum, Alice, and me. Our dad died in a car accident when we were babies. I don't remember him at all but Mum says he was a great guy. I know that's true because my mum wouldn't have picked someone who wasn't. And after all, he's part of Alice and me, isn't he?

Anyway, Alice and I left Mum with a lot of boxes to unpack and went to view the local teen scene. We'd just moved to Somerset from Evanston, Illinois, because Mum got a big promotion at the company where she works. She's a management consultant. Don't ask me what that means because it seems to change from week to week. All I can tell you is that she was thrilled about the promotion and the move.

Seeing as how we were about to be going to a new school, I was *not* all that thrilled. I thought starting senior school was going to be hard enough without having to do it in a brand new school where neither one of us knew a soul.

But the way Alice saw it, she thought it could maybe work out better that way. "Think of it like this," she said. "When you start senior school with a group of people you've known since kindergarten, you're with people who have seen you throw up at break and bawl because you didn't get to be a fairy in the school play. How can you feel like a sophisticated teenager under those circumstances?"

She crossed her arms and began to pace. "The kids at Somerset High have never seen us with braces. Never seen us in polyester cowgirl outfits. Never seen us with that strange crust we used to get around our noses when we had colds. That means that from now on, we can be anything we want to be. Go by nicknames. Dress hip. Be the ultimate in teenage coolitude."

She had a point. She definitely had a point.

We gave a lot of thought to nicknames. Alice was partial to "Spike" and "Blanco". I thought those names were too heavy on the heavy metal overtones. I preferred names that had more dignity. Names like "Muffin" and "Pooky".

We never could agree so we forgot about the nicknames and decided to concentrate on clothes.

That's what led up to our "spy mission". We'd only been in town for two weeks. Most of that time had been spent unpacking and getting settled into our new house. We hadn't met anybody our own age yet. That was OK. Our plan was to lay back, keep a low profile, and see what kids were wearing in Somerset before we spent a lot of money on our new image.

Now Somerset has many beautiful civic features. But what's really important is that there are six cinemas, two skating rinks, a hamburger joint that looked pretty lively, and a disco. Compared to the little town we'd lived in, Somerset was teen Nirvana.

We staked out the hamburger joint first — strategically placed ourselves on a bench across the street and watched the kids go in and out.

"OK," Alice muttered. "So far I'd say the prevailing fashion trend could be described as an eclectic blend of punk, funk, prep and street."

"I'll take your word for it," I said. "All I can tell you is I don't think we've got anything in my cupboard that looks quite like what they're wearing."

"That's a big affirmative. Right off the top of my head, I'd say we're looking at a complete wardrobe overhaul."

5

"Sounds expensive," I commented.

Alice peeked at me over the tops of her sunglasses and grinned. "Here's our approach."

I started the ball rolling that night at dinner.

"Mum," I said, reaching for a roll, "when you consult with companies, do you ever talk to them about image?"

"Oh, absolutely," my mum said. "Image can very often determine the success or failure of a business."

"When you say *image*," Alice said with big wide innocent eyes, "does that mean how you dress and stuff like that?"

Mum smiled. "That's an over-simplification. But yes, the way people dress when they go to work very often affects the way they are perceived – not only within their own organization, but also by clients and customers."

Alice nodded. "That's true in a school, too. I've noticed that the way kids dress seems to really affect how they fit in and stuff like that."

Mum reached for the broccoli and nodded wisely. "You're right, Alice. Which is why I think school uniforms make so much sense. Uniforms build a sense of unity and reinforce the concept of common goals."

I choked on my milk and Alice looked alarmed. This wasn't where we wanted to take this conversation.

"Ummm, yeah," Alice said quickly. "But they don't wear uniforms at Somerset High."

"I know," Mum said in an absent voice. "It's a shame, too."

Alice kicked me under the table and I jumped in. "But aren't people more productive when they're allowed to develop their potential as individuals?"

"Right," Alice chimed in. "Aren't people better pu . . . I mean *employees*, when they have a good self image as their own person?"

That's when Mum smelt a rat. She looked at me and then she looked at Alice. "What is this conversation about?" she asked suspiciously.

Oh, well. After fourteen years you can't expect them to keep falling for the same old one-two punch.

"Clothes," we said together.

"I thought so. What did you have in mind?"

I knew my mum had had a raise but it must have been better than I realized. She came right up with the cash. Whipped out the old wallet and quibbled not.

So we were armed and dangerous when we got

to the mall. And the Somerset mall was definitely well equipped to meet all our shopping needs. Five boutiques, four shoeshops, six places to eat, and two bookshops.

We checked out one of the bookshops and then we wore out two clerks in the shoeshop. After that we got some ice cream in one of the cafés. Alice immediately made a friend for life out of the waiter by telling him he looked just like Tom Cruise.

"So what do you think?" she asked as we sat there ploughing through a butterscotch sundae with two spoons. "Clotheswise, I mean?"

"I'd say we should shoot for an eclectic blend of funk, punk, prep and street."

"Good choice," she laughed. "But to match or not to match? That is the question."

"I say match. Dressing alike is fun – and besides . . ." I pulled my mouth down at the corners like Mum does when she's trying to make a serious point, ". . . just think what it'll do for our sense of unity and concept of common goals."

Alice laughed so hard she dropped a spoon full of ice cream in her lap. She picked it up and and wiped up the mess with a napkin. "I'm not sure, though, Lily. Do you think matching might seem really . . . young?"

She looked up, and I know she must have seen

the look of disappointment in my face. "What if we match generally but not exactly?" she suggested brightly. "You know, like different colours. Because you're right, if we get the right look pulled together, it'll be twice as effective if we're both wearing it. We want people to notice us, and two is better than one. Always has been."

"Always will be," I put in.

"I mean, we're not going to slink around like wallflowers," Alice continued. "I want us to know everybody and I want everybody to know us."

Her eyes were sparkling with excitement. As usual, her enthusiasm was infectious. I could feel myself getting excited. Like everything else that I did with Alice, school was going to be a blast.

Like I said before, shopping for clothes is not my best sport. So I let Alice do most of the work. We went to a trendy-looking boutique and while she checked out the leather mini skirts, I went over to look at the socks. I was trying to decide between white anklets with green trim, or green anklets with white trim when the sales girl came over and asked if she could help me. Before I could answer, I felt the atmosphere in the shop change. All the teenagers sort of froze and looked towards the door.

I saw immediately what had spooked them – a tall blonde, two brunettes, and a redhead with IN CROWD written all over them.

Don't ask me how I knew they were the in crowd. I knew, that's all. They didn't have an "I" tattooed on their foreheads or anything. It's just a look that "in crowders" always have. Mainly, you know when you're in the presence of an "in crowder", because you feel out.

Alice and I had our social ups and downs in junior school. We had started being out, and finished being in. Mostly we thought it was all a big laugh. In or out, we always managed to have a good time if we were together.

The girls were laughing and looking round the store to see who was there. The tall blonde's eyes flickered past me and then guess what happened? That's right. Alice walked right up to the tall blonde and started smiling and talking. And the tall blonde girl started smiling and talking back.

There are times when I'm just not up to the strain of meeting a lot of new people – especially when they're incredibly gorgeous, cool, popular and possibly brilliant too. So I stepped behind the sock rack and began to make conversation with the sales girl.

"So," I said. "Do you work here full-time or

part-time?" That led to a big discussion about her career plans in the wonderful world of fashion merchandising. She was slowly but surely working her way to the top. She'd already been made head of the sock and accessory department the previous week.

The whole time we were talking, I watched Alice & Co. out of the corner of my eye – while carefully hidden behind the tasteful display of day-glo anklets and novelty shoelaces.

I could see Alice darting glances round the store, looking for me. But I was in my wet mode and didn't come out.

Finally, Alice told them goodbye and came looking for me. When she found me, she grabbed my arm and hustled me out of the shop like she'd caught me stealing. I didn't particularly appreciate it since a) I was still clutching a pair of white anklets with lime-green trim that I hadn't paid for, and b) the salesgirl was just getting to the good part of her life story – the part where she was telling me how much more clever she was than her boss.

"Hey!" I protested. "That girl is the head of the whole sock and accessory department."

"I don't care if she's head of the FBI. We've got to talk. Did you see those girls who came in?"

"The tall blonde, the two brunettes, and the redhead?" I asked.

"Yup."

"No, I didn't see them."

Alice grinned. "Those are the cheerleaders."

"NO! You don't mean it? What a surprise! Never would have guessed it."

Alice giggled and let go of my sleeve. "I think we should give them a run for their money."

"What are you talking about?"

"I'm talking about taking Somerset High by storm. I'm talking popularity. I'm talking dates. I'm talking parties. I'm talking going for the brass ring."

"I still don't know what you're talking about."

"I'm talking about trying out for cheerleader," she said simply.

I opened Alice's mouth and looked inside. "Hello?" I shouted. "Hello . . . Hello . . . Hello." I repeated in a faint voice, pretending to be an echo. Then I shook my head. "I thought so. It's empty. I hate to tell you this, Alice, but you've lost your mind. You want to check the shoeshop? See if somebody found it and turned it in?"

"I haven't lost my mind," she giggled. "I just got all the info. There are two slots open because two girls dropped out over the summer. One girl because she had back problems. And one girl because her family moved. So let's go for it. We've got nothing to lose. It'll be fun."

"Did you tell them you wanted to try out?"

"No. I thought I'd run it by you first. What do you think?"

"Get help. Get it now before it's too late. Today cheerleader. Tomorrow world conquest. Where will it stop, Alice? Where will it stop?"

She choked on a laugh. "Come on, Lily. We were cheerleaders last year."

"That was junior school," I pointed out. "We're talking senior school now. These things are popularity contests. We don't know anybody here. Who would vote for us?"

"Anybody who sees us try out," Alice said. "We're going to be so good at the trials, they wouldn't dare not vote for us. Look, Lily, remember that speech that Mum gave last year at her company's annual meeting? She said the secret to success is think big, be prepared, and don't let yourself be intimidated."

"Thank you, Dale Carnegie," I laughed. But in spite of myself, I was getting a big picture of me and Alice waving pom-poms and having boys stand in line to ask us for dates. Maybe it wasn't so impossible after all.

2

We practised, and practised, and practised. Then we practised some more. I took all the cheers from our old school and rewrote them using the name of our new school. Alice worked up a whole routine complete with tumbling moves.

All things considered, we made a pretty impressive little show. Now we just had to hope it was impressive enough to get us through the cheerleader trials, which, Alice discovered, were being held one week after school started.

We'd been practising all afternoon when, suddenly, Alice decided she had to sit down because she was tired and her head hurt.

But Alice could never sit still for long. She started squinting at me and holding up her hands to frame me like a film director.

"What are you doing?" I asked.

"Trying to figure out how we would look with short hair."

"How short is short?"

"Really short," she said.

"Are we talking a bob or a buzz?"

"A combination. I cut out a picture." She reached in her pocket and pulled out a page from a magazine.

Wow! I was floored. It was totally extreme. In a million years I couldn't imagine getting my hair cut like that. I could see how it might be good on us, though. The model looked quite like we did. Big blue eyes. Heart-shaped face. Brunette. But Alice and I had had long straight hair since we were ten. "I don't know," I said. "It's not really me."

Alice just grinned. "No. But it's *us*."

An hour later I was sitting in a chair at the local chop shop getting the back of my hair shaved and the front cut thick and shaggy.

We were laughing and goofing around and the hairdresser had to stop every few minutes and laugh. Alice had had hers done first and she kept putting her head next to mine to make sure the hairdresser was getting them just alike.

"It's too long on the right side," she told him.

"Leave the man alone, Alice," I said. "You're going to distract him. If he makes a mistake, I might have to start my new school with no ears."

Alice put her hand up to her forehead and sat down in the next chair frowning.

"Hey! I was just kidding. Alice?" I thought maybe I'd hurt her feelings. Sometimes I sound cross when I don't mean to.

"It's OK," she grunted. "I've just got a headache."

"Another one?" Alice had been getting headaches since before the move.

"I'm sorry," she sighed. "I don't know why my head hurts all the time."

The hairdresser hurried off to find Alice some aspirin. While he was gone, I sat there staring into the mirror, looking at the two of us sitting side by side with our matching haircuts.

I didn't have a headache, but my stomach felt tense. Suddenly, it all seemed incredibly overwhelming – new town, new school, new clothes, new haircuts, cheerleader trials. No wonder Alice had a headache. "Let's face it," I said. "This is all pretty nerve-wracking for both of us. We may not be constitutionally suited for senior school. It's making me nervous."

Alice stopped rubbing her head and grinned at me in the mirror. "Don't be nervous. We're going to have the greatest time at school that anybody's ever had. Just stick with me, kid."

She turned towards me and her eyes lit up. "I want us to really have fun, Lily. I can just see the two of us walking down the halls. Really grown up, you know. Cool clothes. Boys talking to us. Everybody saying 'hi'. I can't wait."

And suddenly, neither could I.

The first day of school was tougher than I expected. Almost every single person looked older than we did. And cooler. And hipper. It made me realize how insane it was for us to even think about trying out for the cheerleading squad. I was going to have to have a talk with Alice. Being enthusiastic and ambitious was one thing. Trying out for cheerleading made us look full of – what do you call it? – "hubris". Like in this Greek myth I read where the hero gets all arrogant and full of himself and the gods smack him for it.

I didn't have a single class with Alice all morning. And at lunch time, I went to the cafeteria by myself with my lunch bag.

Now I have to tell you, Alice and I spent all morning on the great lunch bag controversy.

At our old school, the cool kids took their lunches in brown paper bags. The dweeby kids bought the hot lunch – a nutritionally balanced meal thoughtfully planned by Mrs Oliver, the school's sylph-like dietician who weighed eighteen stone at least.

However, we'd had it on good authority from one of our friend's cousins in Cleveland, that it's just the opposite at her school. Dweebs take their lunches. Cool kids buy it.

"I'm taking mine," I announced at breakfast. "We don't know anything about this cafeteria yet. There's no telling what kind of horror they're likely to put on a plate and call food."

"True," mused Alice. "But let's get our priorities straight. You never get a second chance to make a first impression. If lunch bags are uncool, we'll get noticed for the wrong reason. Do you want to come back to our reunion in twenty years and have people say 'Oh yeah, that's Alice and Lily . . . *they brought their lunch*.'"

As usual, she had a point.

"We could put our bags inside our rucksacks," I said. "That way, we can look around and scope out the situation. If it looks like the cool kids have bags, we can whip ours out. If not, nobody ever has to see them."

That's when Mum lost it. She banged down her coffee cup. "For heaven's sake," she exploded. "What possible difference can it make to anyone whether you take your lunch or buy it?"

Parents! They don't know anything and you can't tell them.

The upshot was that Alice and I both left for school with a bagged lunch in our rucksacks, and lunch money in our pockets. Either way, we had it nailed.

On the way into the cafeteria, I saw a hip-looking girl carrying a lunch sack so I figured it was OK to pull mine out. I had just walked through the big double doors when I spotted Alice.

Who was she sitting with? The In Crowd, of course. Four of the girls I recognized from the mall. The Blonde, the two Brunettes and the Redhead. Then there were two other girls I'd noticed in the halls – mainly because they'd been walking with good-looking guys.

They were all incredibly glamorous looking and Alice sat there laughing and talking with them like they were all her best friends. Looking at her objectively, I realized she knew what she was doing with that haircut. It looked totally cool with her denim jacket and long earrings.

She fitted right in. Then I realized that if she looked totally hip, so did I. It gave me a little more confidence.

"Lily," she called out. "Over here!" If it hadn't been for Alice, I would never have had the nerve to speak to those girls, much less plop myself down in a chair next to the Blonde. But I must say, I carried it off pretty well. Sat down just as natural as you please. "Hi," I said, opening my lunch bag in a very exaggerated way and giving Alice a significant look.

Her face squinched up so I knew she was trying not to laugh. "Lily, this is Connie, Beverly, Jackie, Tony, Stacy, and Patty."

I certainly was glad my name ended in an "ie" sound. It was a sign from the gods of popularity. Social success was mine. All I had to do was reach out and . . .

"You're twins!" squeaked Beverly, looking back and forth between me and Alice. "I just realized it."

What a mind!

"So do you two always, you know, dress alike?" asked Stacy, exchanging an amused look with Beverly. There was just the tiniest hint of a sneer in her voice. Maybe Alice and I had goofed. Maybe wearing matching outfits –

even just *generally* matching outfits – was unhip. Uncool. Totally dweeby. Social suicide.

Alice rose to the occasion, no problem whatsoever.

"Of course," she laughed. "If God had meant for us to look different, he would have made Lily a boy."

Ha ha ha ha ha! Everybody giggled and I could feel a little ease in the tension.

"Do you ever fool teachers? You know, take tests for each other?" Jackie wanted to know.

"Depends on how much I pay her," I quipped.

All the girls laughed again and so did I. Ha ha ha ha ha. We were all getting very clubby.

"You two are all right," Stacy says, giving us this nod.

See what I mean? Give Alice two minutes to work the crowd and the audience is right with her. Lunch wasn't even over and we were already warm and fuzzy with the In Crowd.

Connie, the tall blonde, took her food out of the bag and began to arrange it in front of her. "So you two just moved here. What do you think you're going to want to do in the way of extracurricular activities?"

"Same thing we did in Evanston," said Alice airily. "Cheerleading."

Connie jerked her head up. There was a stunned silence. The girls looked totally offended. It was such a faux pas. Alice sounded unbelievably presumptuous – even to me.

I turned chicken. I couldn't watch. The goddesses of popularity sniffed hubris. They'd spotted disrespect and retribution was on the way. I hoped I could avoid it by rooting around in my lunch bag. It was cowardly. But at least I didn't crawl right under the table which was what I really wanted to do.

But Alice just stared right back at them – as if she didn't have any idea that she'd made a blunder. "The trials are next Monday, is that right?" she asked evenly.

What courage! What nerve! What insanity! I wondered if families still kept their loony members in the attic. We had a big attic. Alice would like it up there. I'd be good to her, too. Sit with her in the evenings. Help her make oven gloves out of coloured wool.

Alice and Connie stared at each other like a couple of gunslingers.

Connie blinked first. Then she gave Alice a little tight smile. "Yes," she said. She took a deep breath and then she started talking in this very patient, very kind voice – like she was talking to a child who wasn't too bright. "But as captain of the squad, I think I should tell you that cheerleading is a big *honour* here at Somerset High. You two are new here and . . ." She shrugged. "Let's just say it would be very unusual for two completely new girls to get on the squad."

That was high-schoolese for *this town ain't big enough for the two of us*.

Alice took a bite of her sandwich and chewed thoughtfully. "Well," she chirped merrily. "Nothing ventured, nothing gained."

That *who does this girl think she is* look telegraphed from face to face. I didn't know whether or not Alice saw it. But I did and I could feel my face turning beetroot red.

When lunch was finally over, Alice and I got up and headed out of the cafeteria. As soon as we were back in the hall, Alice grabbed my sleeve. "So what did you think?"

"I think they're going to ride us out of here on a rail," I said.

"No way!" Alice cried. "It's just a test. Don't you get it? They're just strutting their stuff. You know, flexing a little muscle. But we'll show 'em. We'll mop up the floor with the competition. All we've got to do is practise, practise, practise."

23

3

"After we shop, let's try to get in another couple of hours of practise," said Alice.

It was Saturday afternoon and we were on the way to the mall. "How much practising are we going to do?" I demanded. It was getting to where I was hearing cheers in my sleep and the muscles in my legs were constantly sore.

"As much as it takes," she said.

"I don't know about this. It seems like a long shot. Did you know the Somerset squad won the national competition last year? There are pictures of it on the bulletin board in the hall. Connie's holding a big trophy and everybody's standing round her holding certificates."

"Why are you being so negative about this?" she said suddenly, in a cranky tone of voice.

"I'm not being negative. I'm trying to be realistic."

"You *are* being negative. We can do everything those other girls can do. And we can probably do it better. Why do you have to be so insecure all the time?"

She sounded really angry and there was a little break in her voice like she wanted to cry.

It took me by surprise. I was the usually the moody one. Not Alice. It was also unusual for Alice to come down on me like that. She was always my biggest fan.

It hurt my feelings and it must have showed in my face because she put her hand to her head and started to rub it. "I'm sorry. I'm sorry. I didn't mean to bite your head off. I've got a headache and it's making me grouchy."

A headache again. Whether she would admit it or not, Alice was feeling stressed. A lot of it was my fault. Here she was, knocking herself out to make sure we got the most out of school, and instead of helping her, I was dragging my feet and complaining.

She put her arm round me. "Please don't be angry. I don't know why I'm being so hard to get along with."

"Would you cut it out," I begged, feeling guilty

25

as anything. "You're not being hard to get along with. You're never hard to get along with. If you don't believe me, look at how well we get along."

She laughed and her face relaxed. I threaded my arm through hers. "You're right. I am sounding negative. Whether we make the squad or not, it'll be fun to try out and at least we'll get noticed."

"Hey, Alice!" I heard behind us.

We both turned and saw this really good-looking guy walking towards us. I'd seen him in the hall several times. You couldn't help but notice him. He was tall and blond, and he had that kind of skin that always looks tanned.

Alice took a deep breath and – presto – the headache look was gone. "Smile," she hissed at me out of the corner of her mouth. "He's older than us."

"You know him?" I hissed back.

"I've talked a couple of times. Now *smile* and don't wimp out," she ordered.

I smiled. I smiled big.

"Hi, Jason," she said, cocking her head sideways like she was getting ready to pound water out of her ears. I wondered if I should cock my head sideways too. Nahhhh! We didn't want to give him vertigo.

Jason gave us both a friendly, but shy, smile. "This is the first time I've seen you two right next to each other." He shook his head. "Truly amazing."

We both grinned. It's fun when people notice how much alike we look.

"How are you doing? Finding your way around town OK?"

"Oh, sure," Alice smiled. Boinnnggg! Her head flopped over and bounced over her other shoulder. It made her hair do interesting things. I made a mental note to cultivate this mannerism at the earliest possible opportunity. "This is my sister, Lily."

Jason grinned but seemed to be at a loss for words. Not to worry. Alice jumped right in. The next thing I know, the three of us are walking towards the mall. Alice is gabbing away about school and sports and films – drawing Jason out. Before you know it, Jason is getting pretty talkative and even *I* am in there yakking away like I've known Jason since nursery school.

Finally, Jason stopped. "Hey," he said with a laugh. "You two got me so interested in talking I came three blocks too far."

We all stood at the intersection. "There's a party tonight at Karen Ann Cooperman's house. If you'd like to go, I'll stop by and walk you over. It'll give you a chance to meet some people."

"That sounds great," Alice said.

It sounded great to me too.

Jason stuck his hands in his pockets. "All right! I'll see you at about eight o'clock then. You're in that brick house with the low hedge out front, right?"

"Right!" we said together – creating a stereophonic effect for his listening pleasure.

"It's a date then. I'll see you later." Jason crossed the street.

As soon as he was out of earshot, Alice let out an excited screech. "This is great! A party. This is the ultimate. CAN YOU BELIEVE IT?"

No. I couldn't. It had all happened so fast. One minute we were two ordinary but ambitious new girls. The next minute, we were poised on the brink of social success. It was too awe-inspiring for words.

"Let's try it again!" Alice said. "I'm OK now."

"Enough already! We've been practising for two hours. This is the second time you've had to stop because you're dizzy. And you're holding your head like it hurts."

"I'm fine," she insisted. "Let's just try it one more time."

"If we get too tired, one of us is liable to get hurt." We were incorporating a lot of gymnastics into our routine. When you get tired, you get sloppy. When you get sloppy, you get hurt. It was hot outside and Alice's face was looking pale. "Besides," I added, "we've got to start getting ready for the party."

"I promise this is the last time." She raised her hands over her head and prepared to do a cartwheel. Instead, she bent over double and started throwing up.

I was stunned. It was so sudden I couldn't think what to do. Mum must have been watching us from the window because she came running out with a wet towel. Alice stopped being sick, heaved a little, and then started crying. Mum hustled her into the house and got her into bed.

"But I can't have the flu!" Alice moaned. "Not tonight. We're going to a party."

"I'll call and cancel," I said. "I'm sure Jason will ask us to another party sometime."

Alice sat straight up in bed and glared at me. "Don't you dare cancel. You go to the party. That way you can tell me all about it."

"By myself!" I yelped.

"You're not going by yourself. You're going

with Jason." She smiled. "Just you and Jason. Like a date."

"Whoaa," I said, getting nervous. "It's not a date."

"It's a date."

"It is not," I yelled.

She flopped back on her pillows and moaned.

"OK! OK! If it makes you happy, we'll consider it a date. I suppose strictly speaking, it is a date. One guy. One girl. A party."

"A party at a fifth-year's house," Alice said, beginning to look excited in spite of the fact that her face was a greyish green. "Wear the denim mini and the long silver earrings. It'll look so cool when you're dancing. I can see you now . . . lots of people standing around you and laughing."

"Oh, great. Lots of people standing around laughing at me."

"Not *at* you. Laughing at things you say. Because you're funny."

"Aw shucks," I said, pretending to blush. "You're just saying that because we're twins and it's in the contract."

She chuckled. "See! You are funny. Just act natural when you get there. You'll be a smash. It's still pretty warm so I'll bet the party's outside."

She settled herself against the pillows and started

talking, imagining this incredibly sophisticated party at which I am the centre of attention and the object of everybody's admiration.

It was good stuff. So good she got *me* believing it. *Sure*, I thought, *why couldn't it all work out the way she imagined?* All I had to do was be funny, look seductive, act natural – and keep smiling.

I felt so great while I got dressed, I forgot she wasn't going.

The doorbell rang and then it hit me. I felt like an understudy going on for the big star. A cop going into a dangerous situation with no back-up. A skydiver jumping out of plane with no parachute. A . . .

"Why are you just standing there?" Alice demanded, interrupting my thoughts. "Go and answer the door. No, *WAIT*!"

I froze.

Alice sat up and closed her eyes. "Stop and enjoy it, Lily. You're just about to go out on your first date. How do you feel?"

How did I feel? Thrilled to death and tickled pink. If I hadn't been so happy, I would have puked.

4

I wish I could say that my first date was this incredibly romantic evening. A meeting of minds. A melting of hearts. Two souls joined by destiny in Karen Ann Cooperman's finished basement.

Mostly it was awkward pauses and standing around watching other kids watch each other.

At first I worried that Jason would be unhappy because Alice wasn't along.

Then I worried that maybe he would think that Alice and I had engineered the whole situation because I had a crush on him.

Then I worried that . . .

Oh, never mind. You get the idea. Sue me. I'm a worrier.

Turns out I didn't need to worry about any of that stuff. Jason definitely liked me. I stopped worrying about that right away. He got me sodas and danced with me and all that.

It was the conversational aspect of the date that was the problem. Without Alice around, neither one of us seemed to be able to come up with anything to talk about. I made a couple of feeble jokes. He laughed politely. After that, it was tough going. I decided that if I never had another date again, that was fine. It was just too stressful.

Oddly enough, it didn't seem to bother him. He smiled a lot and whenever the awkward pauses got too awkward, he made another run for sodas.

Connie and the rest of the squad were all there. They were friendly and they all asked about Alice. I explained that she had some kind of bug.

One of them said there was a lot of that going around.

Somebody else said, yeah, there really was a lot of that going around.

After that, the conversation kind of went nowhere.

Boy, did I wish Alice were there.

Finally, after about a hundred hours, the party was over and Jason walked me home. He even held my hand – which at that point was really sweaty and probably had all the erotic charm of a sea slug.

At the front door, there was one final awkward pause. Then he took the plunge.

I wish I could tell you my first kiss was really wonderful. A shower of sparks. A display of fireworks. A train barrelling through a tunnel.

Mostly, it was wet. And I was way too nervous to put into practice all the techniques that Alice and I had so carefully studied and discussed.

When I went into the house, I felt strange. I'd had a date. And Alice hadn't. I'd been kissed. And Alice hadn't. I felt like a thief. Like I'd taken something that really belonged to her. I couldn't enjoy it, because I felt guilty. It's hard to explain.

I went up the stairs and tiptoed into our room. Holding my breath, I eased my way across the floor towards my bed.

"So?" says this wide-awake voice in the dark. "Did he kiss you?"

Alice flicked on the light and we both started laughing.

"How do you feel?" I asked.

"Lots better. Now tell me everything."

I sat on her bed and told her all about the date. Every so often she'd squeal and clap her hands. "The squad was there! . . . You danced *two* slow dances! . . . Karen Ann had on a *what*!"

Suddenly, the evening didn't seem so dismal.

When I saw it through Alice's eyes, it seemed wonderful.

I'd been on a date with an older man and gone to a party at the house of an older girl. To top it all off, I'd been kissed.

Wow. What a night! I just had to experience it with Alice before it seemed real.

Alice slept late the next day. Mum told me to stay out of our room and not wake her up. I finished some homework and then I spent the rest of the morning helping Mum unpack boxes of miscellaneous junk.

We were going through the last box when Mum let out a happy shriek. "Here they are. Here they are. Oh, thank heavens. I thought they were gone for good."

The way she was carrying on, I thought she'd found something valuable. But it wasn't jewellery or anything like that. It was a big box of photographs that Mum had taken over the years.

"I never found them when we were packing. I thought that somehow they'd been thrown out. But the box was mixed up with all these old files."

She opened the box and inside it there were hundreds of photographs. "I've been meaning to get these put into albums for years. But I've never had the time.

"Look at this one!" She handed me one of the pictures and I cracked up. It was a picture of me and Alice sitting in a little plastic pool in the garden. We had on matching swimsuits and we were both wearing little flippers and masks.

She pulled another one out of the box and smiled, handing it to me to look at. "I've always loved this picture of you. You look so pretty in that sweater."

I remembered the picture. It was of me standing by myself in the garden of our old house. It had been taken last summer. I didn't like it as much as Mum did. I couldn't put my finger on it, but something about that picture bothered me and made me feel sad. Maybe it was because almost all the pictures were of Alice and me together, and this one was of me by myself.

"Look at this one!" Mum giggled. She handed me another picture and we both started laughing hysterically. It was a picture of me and Alice dressed up like Raggedy Ann and Raggedy Andy for Hallowe'en.

Mum and I spent an hour looking through those pictures. I had so much fun, I almost forgot about the big knot in my stomach. It was only when we found the picture of me and Alice in our junior school cheerleader uniforms that I remembered why I had a knot in my stomach.

The cheerleader trials were tomorrow. By tomorrow afternoon, Alice and I were going to be heroes – or else we were going to look like the biggest fools in the history of South Somerset High.

"We won't be home until about five," Alice told Mum at breakfast. "The cheerleader trials are today."

Alice grinned at me and I did my best to smile back. It wasn't easy, though. I'd never felt less like grinning in my life. What I felt like doing was barricading myself in the garage until graduation.

I'd had anxiety dreams all night last night. In one dream, we forgot the words to all the cheers during the try-out. In another dream, we couldn't find the football field. We were running round and round the school, but we just couldn't find where we were supposed to be. There was even one dream where just before we were about to try out, Alice disappeared and I couldn't find her.

Mum looked up from the paper. "Now listen, Alice, I don't want you to get your hopes up too high over this. You two are in a new school and you can't expect to fit in right away."

My sentiments exactly.

But Alice just winked at me across the table.

"Man! These girls are lame!" I snorted. We'd seen six girls try out and maybe two were coordinated enough to walk and chew gum at the same time. I was beginning to feel better about our chances. Alice and I were sitting in the stands waiting for our turn. We were up last. Around us, there were about twenty teachers. The rest of the audience was made up of kids.

"We're going to blow the competition out of the water," Alice said confidently.

Down on the field, Captain Connie was whipping her clipboard around like General MacArthur. She made a couple of notes on it and then looked in our direction. "Alice O'Neil and Lily O'Neil."

Alice slapped my palm. "Let's do it!" she said.

What can I tell you? We were great. It was like something out of a film. The minute we started our routine, we could feel the audience wake up and get excited. We jumped. We tumbled. We break-danced. Our splits were masterpieces of synchronized gymnastics.

When we finally did our last split, the stands erupted into a standing ovation.

Alice and I high-fived each other and then we took a bow. Even Captain Connie was applauding.

Things finally settled down and Alice and I went back to our place on the bench and wiped our faces with towels.

"What do you think?" I asked.

Alice gave me a huge grin. "Even if we don't make it, I still feel great," she said. "We were really a team out there."

I grinned back. "We really were, weren't we?"

Captain Connie and a couple of the other cheerleaders came right over. "Great work!" Connie laughed. "I thought you two were all talk. But I was wrong."

"So are we on the squad?" asked Alice bluntly.

"Starting right now," Connie said.

All the other cheerleaders began to applaud.

Connie tore off a couple of sheets of paper and handed us each one. "This is the meeting schedule. Miss more than five meetings and you're out."

She handed us another couple of sheets of paper. "This is the game schedule. Miss more than two games, and you're out."

She handed us another couple of sheets of paper.

"This is the code of conduct expected from a cheerleader. Step out of line and . . ."

". . . we're out," I finished for her. I clicked my heels and gave her a salute.

Alice shot me a dirty look but Connie wasn't offended at all. She thought it was funny. "OK," she laughed. "I get a little carried away but I just want you to understand that we're really proud of our squad. We want you to be proud of it too – and proud of yourselves." She shook her head as if she couldn't quite believe it. "You two are really something."

Suddenly, she looked different. Not threatening at all. When she dropped the boot-camp stuff, she was pretty likeable. "We still have to get the faculty recommendations. Don't worry. It's a formality. Nobody even came close to you two."

Alice and I high-fived each other again and the cheerleaders all laughed.

Then I high-fived Connie and the next thing, we were all bumping our hips together and shouting the chants and having a ball. I knew then that senior school was going to be a thousand megaton blast.

"You two are going to be fun," Tony said to me, as if she were reading my mind. "I can tell already." She looked round at all the other girls.

"Let's drop our stuff at the gym and go and get something to eat."

"Great idea," Connie said. "Let's go."

People were starting to come down out of the stands then, and everybody was slapping us on the back and saying congratulations.

Jason came over and gave me a big smile. "That was great!" he said. "How did you two learn to do all that stuff? You looked like gymnasts out there."

"We did a lot of gymnastics at primary school," I explained. "And we were cheerleaders in junior school." We talked for a few more minutes and I told him about some of our zanier junior school exploits.

"So where is Alice, anyway?" he asked.

That's when I realized we were practically the last people standing around the stands. I looked over and saw the cheerleaders walking across the field on their way back to the gym.

Alice and Connie were walking with their heads together and laughing. The other girls were walking behind them. Beverly said something to Alice, and Alice looked back over her shoulder and said something that made Beverly laugh. Tony did a little dancing step that brought her up level with Alice and she put her arm through Alice's. They all looked so natural together. So happy and at ease. It was like they'd all been hanging around together for years.

All of a sudden, I got scared. Alice wasn't just my sister. She was my best friend in the whole world. What if she got so friendly with the other girls that she didn't want to spend as much time with me?

It was a horrible, depressing thought.

But then Alice stopped and looked round – like she'd forgotten something important back at the stands. I wondered what she was looking for.

And then I realized, she was looking round for *me*. As soon as she spotted me, she started frantically waving her arms around and making silly faces – like she was saying *Come on. Hurry up. Come and be with me.*

I'll never forget the way she looked standing there in the middle of the field, the late afternoon sun shining down on her hair while she waved her hands around and made me and everybody else laugh.

And I'll never forget the way it made me feel. Proud that we were twins. Proud that she was my best friend. Proud that she was looking for me. *Me.*

I was so relieved and happy to know that Alice

hadn't forgotten about me that I started running towards her. I didn't even say goodbye to Jason or anything. I just ran to catch up with Alice – afraid that if I didn't hurry, she might leave without me.

I woke up on the morning of our first game feeling like I had the world by the tail.

It was just a practice game but Connie wanted us to integrate into the squad as soon as possible. We'd been practising with them every afternoon and we'd learned most of the cheers, although there were still some moves we weren't one hundred percent together on.

We'd driven Mum crazy, making her rush around buying our uniforms and stuff. She'd had to stay up all night two nights in a row getting the hems taken up. Say what you will, Mum comes through when you need her.

I bounced out of bed and did a couple of stretches. "Today's the day!" I said to Alice, who was still buried under the covers. "Rise and shine! Stand up and cheer!"

Alice moaned and stuck her face out from under the covers. "I'm ill," she said in a little sad voice.

My heart stopped. "Oh, no," I said.

"My head hurts and I feel dizzy and nauseous," she whispered.

"Please don't do this to me!" I begged.

"I can't help it," she sniffed. Then she began to cry.

"Alice," I pleaded. "Pull yourself together. You can't back out on me today."

She let out a whimper and pulled the covers around her closer.

I ran to the door. "Mum!" I yelled. "Alice is ill. Come and do something!"

No way did I feel up to handling the big event on my own. One thing I'd noticed during practice – when Alice was around, I felt like one of the group. When Alice wasn't around, I didn't. I felt like an outsider.

But I had to go. Mum insisted and so did Alice. I knew it was going to be awful the minute I got there.

There were a million kids around the school and only two or three faces looked familiar. Who were all these people anyway?

Without Alice, I felt outnumbered and over-whelmed. I also felt shy and conspicious. Even though I heard an occasional voice say "Hi, Lily!", I kept my eyes on the ground until I got to the football field.

I could hear the band warming up and saw the

guys on the team standing around the sidelines bending and stretching and warming up. As I walked past them to get to the squad, I realized that I didn't know one single guy on our team. Not one.

Connie and the squad were standing in a huddle. Stacy spotted me first. "Here they are!" she shouted.

"Where's Alice?" demanded Connie.

"She's got the flu," I said.

There was a big group sigh of disappointment. Hey! I knew I was no substitute for Alice. But they didn't have to rub it in.

I was being oversensitive. But so what? I was entitled, wasn't I? I mean, I'd never signed on as a solo act.

Connie blew the whistle and started clapping her hands. "Line up!" she shouted. "They're doing the toss."

When I looked up into the stands and saw all those hundreds of kids watching me, I realized I'd rather be facing a firing squad. My legs began to shake like jelly.

Tony shook my arm and giggled. "Don't be nervous. The whole point is just to have a good time."

★

Let me tell you something. Tony didn't know anything. Captain Connie took what she did very seriously and she was on my back from the word go. I made the line look ragged. I wasn't shouting loud enough. My smile looked insincere. (NO KIDDING!) I thought the game would never be over. By halftime, I hated her guts.

"Look," Connie said to me as the team ran for the stands. "I know you're probably nervous today, but the best thing you can do is just get out there and have a good time." (Why did everybody keep saying that?)

I nodded and didn't say anything. There was a lump in my throat and I was afraid I'd cry if I tried to talk.

Then Connie bumped her hip against mine and I stopped hating her. She was just trying to do her job. The hip bump was her way of telling me not to get all bent out of shape.

"You can do it, Lily," she said. Then she walked away blowing on her whistle in case somebody might forget she was the captain or something.

Tony and Stacy were standing behind me and I could hear them giggling. "Don't get all excited about Connie," Tony said. "She takes this stuff a little too seriously sometimes. She's a real perfectionist. She made the two of us miserable last year. It paid off, though. We were national champions."

They invited me to go with them to the refreshment stand and we started to talk. After a while, I felt more relaxed. I got through the second half of the game and believe it or not – I almost had a good time.

Connie had a couple of nice things to say to me afterwards, and Tony invited me to go with them to get something to eat. What I really wanted to do, though, was get home and see how Alice was doing. I knew she'd be waiting for a full report.

5

Mum took Alice to the doctor on Monday morning, and I went to school. There was a cheerleaders'
meeting after school and Alice was determined to
get there. "He'll thump me, look in my ears, and
then tell Mum to stop being such a worrier,"
she said. "I should be at school by lunch time at
the latest."

But I didn't see Alice at lunch. By the time I
walked into the meeting room (which was an
empty classroom off the main hall), it was obvious
that Alice wasn't going to show up. I wondered
if Mum had made Alice go back to bed after her
doctor's appointment.

The meeting was mainly about game schedules
and things like that. Connie gave everybody a little
critique. She said a few nice things about my debut

performance and everybody applauded. Tony and Stacy spent a lot of time giggling and Connie spent a lot of time telling them to shut up. After that, we went over some new cheers and the meeting was over.

As we were walking out, Tony pulled on my arm. "Come and keep me company," she said. "I've got to pick up some stuff in the yearbook committee room."

"You're on the yearbook committee?"

She nodded. "Yeah. I help put out the literary magazine, too. It's the same committee, really. We use the same room and the same equipment. If there's any profit from the yearbook, we use it for the literary magazine. If there's no profit, we try to get companies to donate money for the magazine."

I was really surprised when we walked into the room. Tony spent so much time giggling it was hard to take her seriously. But the stuff she was in charge of looked impressive and professional. She showed me how they did the art for the ads and some sample yearbook pages.

"It's a mess now," she said. "But we work all year putting it together. By May, this is what it looks like." She showed me a copy of last year's yearbook and literary magazine. They were beautiful.

"We always need help on the yearbook," she said. "Think you might like to work with us?"

I thought about it for a minute. It actually seemed sort of cool to me. But I really couldn't see Alice wanting to work on something like that. She was more action oriented.

"Thanks," I said. "But I think we'll have enough to do with the cheerleading squad."

"Sure." She nodded. "But let me know if you change your mind."

When I got home that afternoon, my mum's car was gone. I let myself into the house and looked around. There was nobody home. It was the first time I'd been in this house all by myself and it gave me a spooky feeling.

Usually I could hear Alice banging around upstairs or Mum yelling about something. Now, it was completely silent.

Then I heard the front door open. The minute I saw Mum's face I knew something was wrong. She wasn't crying, but she was white as a sheet and her face had an odd, blank look.

"Where's Alice?" I asked in alarm.

"Alice is in St Stephen's hospital, Lily. They're running some tests and . . ."

50

"What kind of tests?" I demanded. "What's going on? I thought she had flu."

Mom held up her hand, telling me to stay cool. "It looks like there could be some sort of a neurological problem," she said lightly.

"Neurological? As in *the brain*?"

"Now listen, Lily," she started. "There's no sense in getting all worked up at this point . . ."

I can't remember what all she said. She was trying to be comforting and I was trying to believe her. I sat on the sofa for a long time feeling stunned and numb. It was hard to believe there might be something seriously wrong with Alice. Just plain unthinkable.

I went back to the hospital with my mum that evening. As soon as we walked in, a gaggle of doctors converged on Mum. She told me to go on to Alice's room while she talked to the doctors.

I found the room and when I opened the door, Alice was sitting up in bed like she'd been waiting for me.

"Alice?"

"What happened at the cheerleader meeting?" she asked.

"Who cares? What's going on? Are you OK? Tell me what they said."

"They said there's something wrong with my brain." She giggled and rolled her eyes. "Like we didn't know *that* already."

"Cut it out, Alice," I said nervously. "Tell me what's going on."

"They're talking brain tumour," she said in this real wise-guy voice.

I was trying hard not to panic. "But what does that *mean*?"

"I think it means I wasted forty bucks on this haircut. Stick around and you can watch them shave my head for surgery."

She tried to grin, and she almost managed to pull it off. She got the corners of her mouth turned up. But then her lips began to tremble with the effort. Her head started shaking and she burst into tears. "Oh, Lily!"

I ran over and put my arms round her, telling her not to cry and that everything was going to be all right. And then, tower of strength and support that I was, I burst into tears myself.

I met Rusty Feller later that night. I first saw him standing in the hall talking to my mum and some lady named Andrea Shepherd who turned out to be a social worker. The hospital had called her and asked her to come over. She'd brought Rusty with her and you never saw such a nerd in your life. Red hair. Rabbity-looking eyes. Tall and skinny. *Yuck!* I'm thinking.

They were both from Hope House, which is a high-tech infirmary for kids about a mile from the hospital. Andrea Shepherd lives there as the resident social worker and Rusty is a part-time male nurse. On his time off, he "familysits" (his euphemism, not mine) for families in our situation. Mum introduced them both to me and the next thing I know, Mum's handing Rusty the house keys and telling him how to work the alarm system.

When I finally realized that they were planning to send me home with this bozo while Mum stayed at the hospital, I flipped. First of all, I didn't want to go home. I wanted to stay there with Alice. Second of all, what did we know about this guy, anyway? He was a total stranger. He could have been a serial killer. A deranged maniac. A terrorist guerrilla.

That's when Mum cracked. She actually started shouting at me right there in the hall. Telling me how she didn't have time for my nonsense right now. That if I was as grown up as I claimed to be, then I should prove it and stop acting like a spoilt child.

It was so out of character, my jaw dropped. I

couldn't believe Mum would actually yell at me at a time like this.

Under the circumstances, I did the only thing I could reasonably be expected to do. I burst into tears again.

Andrea jumped in like somebody breaking up a dog fight. She managed to get everybody calmed down – reminding us that Alice was just down the hall and could probably hear us, and that it was important not to upset her.

"But she's my sister," I kept saying through my sobs. "She's my sister. I want to stay. She's my sister!"

Andrea put her arm round my shoulder and started talking to me. Telling me how the best thing I could do was cooperate with my mum because she was going to have a lot of decisions to make over the next day or so. If I would just be patient, my mum would answer all my questions. But right now I was going to have to trust in her and the staff at St Stephen's to do all the right things.

And that's how I wound up at home being babysat by a completely nerdy red-headed male nurse who couldn't take two steps without tripping over his shoelaces. Needless to say, he didn't inspire confidence.

I'm ashamed of myself when I think of it now. I don't know what got into me. I was so upset and angry about everything, I decided that if they were going to treat me like a child, I was going to act like a child. I pouted all the way home in the car and wouldn't speak to Rusty at all.

"Lily," he said the next day with this great big smile. "If there's anything you want to do, just let me know. Would you like to go to a film? Or get a video out?"

"No," I groaned from the sofa. My mum's big quilt was wrapped round me, and I had collected every pillow in the house and built a pillow fort round myself.

"Well then, what do you want for lunch? We can send out for something. Pizza? Chinese? You name it."

Did he really think I could get interested in food at a time like this?

"Listen," he said. "If you want to have a couple of your friends over, that's fine. Maybe you should do that. No sense in moping around here by yourself."

That did it. The guy was a boob. A total jerk. I was so mad I couldn't see straight. I jumped up, grabbed the quilt and started screaming. "I

DON'T HAVE ANY FRIENDS, YOU STUPID IDIOT!"

Then I ran upstairs and stayed in my room for the rest of the day.

Rusty came up and knocked a couple of times. "Lily," I heard him say in this grotesquely nice tone of voice. "Anything you need or want, let me know. OK?"

"GET AWAY FROM MY DOOR!" I shouted. Jerk!

Mum called at about four that afternoon. She sounded exhausted but she said Alice came through the operation fine.

"When can I come and see her?" I asked.

"In a couple of days, Lily," she said. "She needs some time to recuperate. For now, just try to go on with your normal routine if possible."

"Can't I come and at least visit?" I begged.

"Not now, sweetie. Believe me, it'll be a lot more helpful if you wait a couple of days."

"But, Mum . . ."

"NO!" she practically shouted.

I could feel myself starting to cry like a real baby. I know it wasn't fair to her. She was under a lot of pressure. But I felt so alone and worried I wanted to die.

"Please don't cry, darling. I know this is a tough time. But everything's going to be OK. Just try to put up with it a little longer. Please, Lily?"

"OK," I croaked. Then I got off the phone and let Rusty talk to her.

I went in the living room and cried. A few minutes later, Rusty was sitting next to me and patting me on the back.

Just to let you know how miserable I was at that particular moment in time – I was actually glad to have him around.

I decided to stay home from school again the next day. It felt kind of momentous – making a decision like that all by myself and not checking it out with a grown-up. But I just couldn't go. I was on the verge of hysteria, and there was no way I was going to risk losing it at school.

"Aren't you going to school?" Rusty asked when I came down to breakfast in my nightgown.

"No," I said, reaching for the cereal. "I don't think I am."

He looked confused for a minute. I could just see him thinking. Trying to decide whether or not he could make me go. I gave him the Captain Connie look – that bad gunslinger stare.

His Adam's apple moved up and down a

couple of times. "Do you have any tests today or anything?" he asked. Frowning. Trying to look parental. Oh, please!

I just glared at him.

"OK," he said. "I'll call the school and explain."

I spent the day in my nightgown sitting on the sofa with ten pillows round me and watching television talk shows. *Women who love their pets more than their kids. Satanic lyrics in rock and roll.*

Somewhere between *Poltergeists who look like cartoon characters* and *men who wear pillbox hats* I remembered that there was a cheerleaders' meeting that afternoon. In the big scheme of things, it didn't seem too important.

6

To cut a long story short, the tumour was malignant – in other words, cancerous. That meant that even though the surgeon removed about ninety percent of the tumour, we still had a long way to go with treatment.

Mum and I took Alice to Hope House about a week after her surgery so she could start radiation. Rusty had told me a little bit about Hope House. It was an infirmary, but it was also a hospital annexe for kids who need long-term treatment.

Alice was still weak after her surgery. And as we walked down the halls, neither one of us came up with one joke. Not one. It was so overwhelming, we instinctively reached out and held hands.

We found Alice's room and Mum went to take care of the paperwork. Alice and I sat down on the two beds and stared at each other. "Did you see all those labs we walked by?" Alice asked finally.

I nodded.

"Think they're working on a Frankenstein's monster in this place?"

Before I could answer, there was a voice at the door. "Welcome to Hope House," said this nice-looking lady. She breezed in and shook hands with both of us. "I'm Doctor Lilly Gordon. I'm the oncologist here so you and I are going to be seeing a lot of each other," she said to Alice.

She turned to me and smiled. "And you're Lily. Nice to meet a fellow Lily. But you're Lily with one L and I'm Lilly with two."

"Is this Alice?" said another voice from the doorway.

We all looked up again and saw this gorgeous Afro-American doctor in a white coat giving us a big smile. "I'm Steven Rhodes," he said. "But everybody here calls me Doctor Steve."

"When they're not calling him something worse," a young-looking man said as he came in behind Dr Steve. He had a big booming laugh, which made everything he said sound funny. "I'm Dr Harding, by the way. I heard we had some twins around. Now listen," he warned. "I grew up with twin sisters so don't think I don't know the tricks of the twin trade."

"What does that mean?" Alice giggled.

"It means if you're planning to give anybody a hard time, pick on him," Dr Rhodes said with a laugh. "He's the new guy. That's what he's here for."

Alice and I laughed.

"This is a medical care ward, as you can see," Dr Steve went on, "but I want you both to take a full tour later on because there's more to Hope House than labs and medicine cabinets."

I realized this place wasn't going to be so bad after all. These doctors seemed more relaxed and friendly than the ones at the hospital. Maybe it's because Hope House is just for kids, and they were all trained to deal with people our age. The knot in my stomach began to ease up a little bit. For the first time since that Monday afternoon that I came home and found nobody there, I began to believe that everything was going to be OK.

I saw Rusty again that afternoon. He was walking down the hall with a tray full of little bottles. I held my breath and waited for him to fall over his own feet and drop the tray.

Rusty had been unbelievably clumsy when he'd

stayed at our house. He'd tripped over every rug, banged his head on every cabinet, and slammed his fingers in every drawer. It was pretty frightening considering the guy was a nurse.

In a million years, I couldn't imagine him nursing somebody back to health. I *could* imagine him accidentally whacking them on the head with a bed pan or puncturing some vital organ with a needle. I wondered if I should start thinking up a plan to bust Alice out.

Oddly enough, he managed to get to the nursing station with the tray, transfer all the bottles on to separate shelves, and efficiently note everything on a chart.

Maybe he'd been clumsy and nervous around me because I'd been so mean. It made me feel bad and I wanted to apologize. I cleared my throat until he noticed me.

When he did, he gave me a big smile – which was very nice of him considering how horrible I'd been. "Hi, Lily! Welcome to Hope House."

"Thanks," I said. "Listen, uh, I'm sorry I acted like such a brat when you stayed with me."

"No problem," he said. "Perfectly understandable. When one member of a family gets ill, it's hard on everybody. You were confused and frightened and angry. Don't worry about it."

Now that he was on his own turf, he was amazingly professional. "So what do you think of Hope House so far? Want a tour?"

I didn't. But I felt like I needed to make up for my behaviour and he seemed to want to give me one. So I let him take me on the grand tour.

Once you got off the ward for the really sick kids, it wasn't like a hospital annexe at all. There was a living room with a fireplace, and a library. Every floor had a couple of sitting rooms and they didn't look institutional at all. They had overstuffed armchairs and big sunny windows that looked out over the garden.

Our last stop was the kitchen. The minute we walked in, I smelt chocolate chip cookies. A nice-looking lady was taking a huge tray of cookies out of the oven.

"Mrs Brady," Rusty said. "This is Lily O'Neil. Her sister is here for radiation and chemo."

Mrs Brady smiled. "Is this one of the identical twins?"

It was nice the way they all knew who we were. Mrs Brady put a plate of cookies on the table and pulled out two chairs. "Now sit down here and tell me what your sister likes to eat."

For the first couple of weeks, Mum let me stay

home from school. We went to Hope House every day and got to know the place even better.

The radiation was tough at first. But Alice maintained her sense of humour even when she was throwing up. Eventually, the nausea got better but she started losing what was left of her hair and getting awful-looking red patches on her scalp.

I did my best to cheer her up and I think I succeeded pretty well most of the time. For the first time in her life, Alice didn't feel like talking, so I'd do silly stuff like turn the TV on with no sound. Then I'd dub in ridiculous dialogue that had nothing to do with the picture.

Alice would get hysterical and sometimes other kids or people from the staff would wander in and listen. Pretty soon, I had a reputation for being a real wit.

The other bed in Alice's room was empty so they let me spend the night a couple of times. Sometimes I talked to other kids in the hall but mostly I stayed in Alice's room and kept her company.

It was hard on Alice. She liked to be up and doing things. Lying around in bed between trips to the radiation lab (or "the plutonium chamber" as we called it) was not her style.

Then one Friday morning at breakfast, Mum

announced that it was time for me to go back to school as of next Monday. She'd be going back to work on something called "flex time". That meant she'd have flexible hours so she could be with Alice when Alice needed her. She said if I wanted to, I could spend the night with Alice that night.

When we went to Hope House later, I had my overnight bag and a couple of old board games we'd brought with us when we moved.

Her door was halfway open and I could hear Alice inside the room talking away. Laughing, too. I hadn't heard her sound so animated since she was first ill.

I thought she was talking to Dr Gordon or Dr Steve. But then I heard a second voice – a young voice. Maybe one of the other kids was visiting Alice.

I pushed the door open and walked in. Imagine my surprise when I saw somebody in *my* bed. I felt like one of The Three Bears – only Goldilocks had no locks at all, gold or otherwise.

There was a bald girl in *my* bed.

"This is my sister, Lily," Alice said. She sounded almost like her old self. "Lily, this is Brenda."

Brenda's face was greyish green. She looked

like she felt awful, but she was smiling anyway. It didn't surprise me. Most people smiled when they were around Alice.

"Brenda's getting chemo," Alice explained. "That's why she feels sick as a dog. She's at Somerset Middle School." Alice chatted on and on about Brenda and how she loved to ride horses and wasn't that great. I nodded and smiled but what I was really thinking is, *what is that girl doing in my bed?*

I kept waiting for Alice to give her a gentle hint that she should clear out and find another place to sleep. But Alice never did.

The door opened and a girl of about sixteen years old came in with a guitar and a handful of bright scarves.

"Hi," she said. "I'm Alison Kim. I'm a volunteer here. I've been off for a few weeks with the flu. That's why I wasn't here to greet you. You're Alice, right?" she said, turning to my sister. "And you're Brenda?" she asked the girl sitting on *my* bed.

They both nodded and I introduced myself.

Alison chatted for a while and then gave Brenda and Alice two matching kerchiefs. The material was cotton with a blue and white cloud motif.

"I made these while I was in bed," Alison

explained with a perky smile. "It made me feel better knowing I was doing something for others. I'd look at the fabric and imagine that I was lying in a field and gazing up at the clouds. Do you lot ever watch the clouds and see how many shapes you can find?"

Her eyes got big and round and her lips formed an "o". It was like a parody of somebody getting a sudden burst of inspiration. Only she was serious. "Maybe when you're feeling blue," she breathed, "you can close your eyes and imagine the clouds are all round your head."

Was this girl for real? What a loon! Alison was a psychiatric case if I ever saw one.

I was waiting for Brenda and Alice to start laughing or yelling for help. But they stayed calm. Didn't even blink.

"It was really nice of you to make these," Alice said, putting hers on. "Thanks."

Brenda put hers on too and smiled.

Alison waved. "I've got some more people to visit but don't worry, I'll be back." She held up her guitar. "And I do take requests – as long as you request Kum Ba Yah."

"Kum Ba *what*!" I said as she left.

Brenda and Alice began to laugh – like they knew something I didn't.

"I'd heard about Alison, but I didn't believe it," Alice giggled.

Brenda fell back on her pillows, laughing. "I believe it now."

"What's going on?" I asked. "Who was that nut-case?"

"That's Alison, the "volunteer from hell". According to the other kids, Alison suffers from terminal perkiness. They humour her though, because they know she means well. They also know they can count on her if they need her. But when they see her with that guitar . . . man! They run. I can see why."

Brenda giggled. "She only knows one song and it's Kum Ba Yah. She's always trying to get people to sing along and nobody ever wants to." She adjusted the kerchief on her head. "It was nice of her to make these. I like mine – a lot." She settled back against her pillows and stared at Alice. "You and I look like twins, now," she laughed.

That's when it dawned on me. That bed wasn't my bed any more. It was Brenda's bed. I wasn't going to be invited to spend the night. If anyone was going to sleep somewhere else, it was going to be me.

Brenda noticed my overnight bag and looked embarrassed. "Were you planning to spend the night?" she asked. "Gosh. I'm sorry. Maybe they can find another room for me."

"Don't be ridiculous," Alice said. "I'll bet Lily's glad she doesn't have to stay here any more. She's probably got a game tomorrow."

"Game?" Brenda asked.

"We're cheerleaders," Alice announced proudly.

"You two are cheerleaders?" Brenda said. "You're kidding!"

She looked back and forth at Alice and me like she'd just found out we were Nobel Peace Prize winners.

Alice told her all about the trials. How we'd done so much work and gone over so big. Brenda wanted to know everything.

"Tell her about the meetings," Alice prompted.

"Well, actually, I haven't been to any meetings lately."

"That's because she's been here with me almost non-stop," Alice explained quickly. Then she turned to me. "But you're starting back at school on Monday, right?"

Don't remind me, I thought. Every time I thought about going back to school without Alice, it just made me sick.

My first Monday back at school was weird beyond

description. It seemed unreal that the whole time we'd been going through a major life crisis, classes had been going on and nothing had changed.

The halls looked and smelt just the same. The same pictures were up on the notice boards. Streams of kids surged through the halls, and all around me I could hear lockers clanging and people talking.

"YO! Willis," somebody yelled. "Think fast."

A ball whizzed past my ear and I saw some guy catch it and lob it back.

How can this be? I thought. How can these people walk around the halls laughing and cutting up and acting like everything is all right when my sister is in Hope House getting radiation treatments for brain cancer? I felt like they didn't care and I hated them for it. It was stupid but I couldn't help it. And I just got more self-righteous as the day went on.

A group of girls were walking behind me on the way to my first class.

". . . Then they told me I had to be home by nine. *Nine!* Can you believe it. They're fascists. My parents are total fascists."

". . . Did you see the assignment Mrs Miles gave us?" another one interrupted. "Can you believe it?"

". . . Jeez!" another girl moaned. "*Twenty pages!* I hate this school."

How dare they complain? I thought. *How dare they gripe?* If they had cancer they'd know what a problem really was.

At lunch time, I went to the cafeteria and saw the squad sitting at their usual table. Tony waved at me and I took my lunch over and sat down.

"Welcome back," she said. "How's Alice? When will she be coming back to school?"

I knew that my mum had called the school to explain where Alice and I had been. The faculty advisers had told Connie there was a problem, but I didn't know how much they all knew and I didn't feel like going into the gory details.

"It'll be a while," I said.

"That's a shame," Connie said. "But tell her not to worry. We'll hold her spot on the squad. There are two alternates who will be happy to sub for her."

The girls all laughed.

"*Happy* is an understatement," Beverly grinned. "They'll be thrilled."

"You'll be at the meeting this afternoon, right?" Tony asked. "I'm really glad you're back. There's a game this weekend at Lafayette. It's about twenty miles north. My dad said he'd drive a bunch of us in his jeep."

"I don't know if I can make it," I said quickly.

71

"Please come," Stacy said. "It'll be fun."

"I said I don't know," I snapped.

The girls all looked surprised and exchanged glances.

"Sure," Connie finally said. "Just let us know. If you have to miss some games, we'll work around it." She squeezed my arm. "Don't worry about it."

Why is it that when people are nice and understanding, it's more upsetting than if they were mean and demanding?

I stood up quickly and hurried out. I managed to get to the bathroom and lock myself in a cubicle just in time.

It's hard to cry silently. Really hard. You have to stuff a lot of your hand in your mouth. Then your teeth make red marks all over your knuckles. When you look at your hand and see the marks, you feel even sorrier for yourself.

Somebody came in the bathroom and I heard a knock on the door of the stall. "Lily?"

It was Tony. "Lily," she said again. "Will you please come out?"

I didn't answer. I couldn't.

"Please, Lily. There's nobody out here but me. Come out."

I tried to get a grip on myself and opened the door of the cubicle. Tony looked concerned.

"I'm OK," I said in this defensive voice.

She bit her lip. "Listen, I know you're new and all. But we're your friends. We'd like to be, anyway. So if there's anything we can do, let us know. OK?"

"OK," I nodded.

"So will you be at the meeting this afternoon?"

"I don't think so," I answered.

"Listen, if you really don't feel like going to the meeting, Stacy and I could skip it this afternoon. The three of us could go out and get a soda or something."

"Thanks," I sniffed. "But I need to go to Hope House."

She chewed on her lip for a minute, looking worried about me. "Doesn't it get depressing for you to be there so much? Don't you sort of dread having to go?"

I just stared at her. She didn't understand. She didn't understand at all. And I couldn't make her understand because the way I felt about it didn't really make sense.

All I knew was that I felt safer and more secure being with Alice in the cancer ward of Hope House than I did at home or at school.

I realize it's stupid, but I felt like the more time I spent with Alice, the sooner she'd get well —

because I *wanted* her to get well. I *needed* her to get well. She was my sister. We were twins. I knew I couldn't exist without Alice. So, therefore, she couldn't exist without me. That's why we had to be together as much as possible.

7

"Will you do me a favour?" Alice asked.

"If you're going to ask me to eat your meatloaf for you, the answer is no. This stuff is heinous."

I picked up a forkful and let it fall back on my plate. I kid you not, it sounded like I'd dropped a brick.

It was a week later. As usual, I'd gone to Hope House after school. I'd get there at four thirty and Mum would generally get there by five or five thirty. If she had to work late, I'd have dinner with Alice in her room.

The staff was really nice about bringing extra trays. Mrs Brady had even asked me what my favourite foods were. If she knew I was going to be there, she tried to make something she knew I'd like.

Overall, the food was good – if you didn't count the meatloaf.

"It's not that," Alice said. "It's something else."

"You want me to lend you money? You want me to smuggle you in some beer? You want me to smuggle you in a guy?"

Alice started laughing. So I kept it up. "Now why would you want me to smuggle you in a guy when you've got a hunk like Rusty around?"

She laughed again and shook her head. "I want you to forget I'm ill."

"Huh?"

She sighed. "I don't know what I'm trying to say. I suppose I'm just tired of talking about being ill. Everybody here is ill. Sometimes it seems like that's all anybody talks about. Radiation. Chemo. Throwing up."

"Well, what do you want to talk about?" I asked.

"You never say anything about school. I know it's because you think it'll make me feel bad about missing out. But it won't. Really. I'd rather hear about the squad and the games and the guys than talk about cancer."

"There's nothing to tell," I said.

"Oh, come on."

"I'm serious. What's to tell?"

"What do you mean what's to tell? Tell me about the squad. Tell me about who's doing what. Who's dating who. Is Connie still being such a pain? Is Tony still as dizzy? Has Stacy got her eye on Connie's job? That's the impression I got at the first couple of meetings."

"Really?" This was news to me.

"Sure. Didn't you notice how Stacy is always making suggestions for how to improve the squad? Connie always ignores her and tries to pretend her ideas are bad, even though a lot of the time they're good."

No, I hadn't noticed.

"And what about that guy Bill?"

"Bill?"

"You know. The guy with the blond ponytail who's trying to grow a beard but not having much luck."

"Oh, that guy."

"Haven't you noticed the way he moons after that redheaded girl from our Spanish class?"

"No."

Alice giggled. "He always waits around in the lunch queue until he sees where she's going to sit. Then he takes his tray and walks behind her and accidentally on purpose, bumps her. She turns to see what's going on and he acts like he's surprised to see her. Then he sits down with her." She sighed. "I really miss school."

It was amazing. It was better than a soap opera and I hadn't noticed any of it. It was hard to believe we'd been going to the same school. Typical Alice. You take the most boring situation in the whole world, and Alice could turn it into excitement, adventure, romance and drama. Alice was missing it, and here I wasn't appreciating it at all.

The door opened and Brenda came in. "Hi," she said. Then she climbed into my, I mean – *her* – bed and grinned. "How's school?"

She had the same eager look in her eyes that Alice did. I felt like a total failure because I couldn't think of one exciting thing to tell them. They wanted news from the front and I didn't have any. I really didn't.

Jason had tried to talk to me a couple of times, but I didn't want to talk to him. What if he asked me out? I couldn't cope with the stress. It was just too much to think about and I needed all my time and energy for Alice. So I ignored him. Every time I saw him coming down the hall, I'd look the other way so I wouldn't have to speak.

I spent a lot of time avoiding Connie and Tony, too. I was afraid that they might invite me to do something and I didn't want to do anything with them. I wanted to be at Hope House.

"Oh, you know," I said evasively. "Just the same."

Brenda grinned. "I suppose you take it all for granted. But it sounds exciting to me. I can't wait to start senior school next year."

Then she looked at Alice. "Hey! You and I will be freshmen together. I just realized it. That's great. You are so much fun," she gushed at Alice. "Senior school will be a blast with you."

My heart sank – just plummeted right down into my shoes.

It was true. Alice was probably going to miss most of the school year. She'd be a year behind me next year. And the year after that. And on and on. I'd wind up going to college by myself.

She and Brenda would be new girls together – doing all the things together that Alice and I had planned to do. I remembered Brenda's remark. *The two of us look like twins now.*

It made me feel absolutely furious. Brenda had taken over my bed. Now she was taking over my sister.

I knew if I didn't get out of there, I was liable to say something I'd be sorry for later. So I excused myself and stalked out.

I was still fuming when Rusty tapped me on the shoulder. "Will you do me a favour?"

I was beginning not to like that phrase. "Depends on what it is," I answered.

"Will you finish a game of fish with Susannah?"

"Who's Susannah?"

He crooked his finger. "I'll introduce you."

I followed Rusty down the stairs to the ground-floor sitting room. There was this little girl sitting at one of the tables looking really peeved. "I've been waiting for you for fifteen minutes," she snapped at Rusty. "Are you in or are you out?"

Whoaaa. I had my own problems. Playing cards with this little brat did not appeal to me in the slightest.

"Listen," I hedged. "My mum's probably going to be here pretty soon and I should really go back upstairs and wait for her."

Susannah gave me this long stare. *She knows I'm lying*, I thought. But that wasn't why she was staring. She points at me and says, "You look just like that girl who hangs out with Brenda. Are you twins?"

What can I say? She'd found the way to my heart. It was so reassuring to know that somebody still recognized us as twins I almost cried. But I didn't. I smiled. "Yeah," I said, sitting down and picking up Rusty's hand. "We're twins. Always have been. Always will be."

"Is it fun to be twins?" she asked.

"It's more fun than anything in the whole world."

Rusty saw his chance to escape and he hurried out, saying he had work to do.

After he was gone, Susannah put her little chin in her hand and looked thoughtful. "I wish I had a twin," she said finally. "Or at least a sister. But I don't. I don't have a brother either. Janet has a big brother. Sometimes he plays with us but if there's a big kid around, he ignores us."

"Who's Janet?"

"Janet is my friend from home. I miss her."

"Where's home?" I asked.

Turns out Susannah was five years old and from a little town in Michigan about three hours north of Somerset. She'd had scarlet fever and it had affected her heart. There were no good medical facilities in her home town and both her parents worked, which is why she was at Hope House. Her folks came to see her every couple of weeks but she was having a tough time of it. Susannah was the youngest patient there and she had nobody her own age to play with.

"Shhhh," she said, tiptoeing to the door.

"What's going on?"

She motioned to me to be quiet. "It's that guy from the second floor. He always comes down here at this time of day. I think it's because he has a crush on the blonde girl."

I went to the door and peeped out over Susannah's head. Sure enough, there was this guy about twelve talking to a girl with a long blonde plait.

"He's here for chemo. She's comes here every afternoon for physical therapy on her leg. Skiing accident," she added. "They did an operation on her knee and now she has to do all kinds of exercises for it."

She watched them for another couple of seconds. "He used to have a crush on Brenda, but she's too old for him. Besides, she spends most of her time with your sister."

"They're pretty good friends, huh?"

Susannah nodded.

I began to see that Susannah might not be a bad person to get to know. It would be like having my own spy right here in Hope House. That way I could keep tabs on the developing Brenda/Alice axis, even though I had to spend most of my time at school.

I felt a little tug on my sleeve and Susannah

pulled me back over to the card table. "There's nothing else to see until six o'clock."

"What happens at six?"

"Dr Graham and Dr Emily always stop in the hall and talk before they leave. I think they're in love."

This kid was great. She was a miniature Alice. She rearranged the cards in her hand and reminded me it was my turn.

"Give me all your fours," I said.

She grinned at me. "Go fish," she said.

A few nights later, I woke up in the middle of the night and couldn't go back to sleep. My stomach felt empty. When it started growling, I decided to go downstairs and get some ice cream.

Strangely enough, Mum was up too. She was sitting at the dining-room table with piles of photographs spread out in front of her. She'd bought a lot of good-looking photo albums and little by little, she was getting the pictures pasted in.

"It's three in the morning," I said. "What are you doing awake?"

"I couldn't sleep," she said. "So I decided to come down and sort through some of these photographs. It gives me something to think about besides work and . . ." She trailed off.

But I knew what she was going to say. She was going to say *"besides Alice"*.

I sat down on the other side of the table and took a really good look at her. For the first time, I noticed she looked old. It wasn't that she suddenly had grey hair or wrinkles. I don't know what it was. She just looked older.

When had it happened? I wondered. When had she started to look different? It scared me. It made me realize that everything was changing round me. I didn't want it to. I didn't want Mum to look old. I desperately didn't want Alice to be ill. I didn't want to go to school day after day by myself. I wanted us all to go back in time and be the way we used to be.

Mum gave me a worried smile. She leant across the table and squeezed my hand. "I think about you, too," she said. "I wouldn't blame you if you felt a little forgotten. Between work and Alice, you and I haven't exactly had any quality time together."

In spite of the way I was feeling, I smiled back. Mum had enough to worry about. She didn't need a big guilt complex over me.

"We'll have it now," I said. "Want some ice cream?"

"Sure," she said with a tired smile. She put the

photographs back in the box and we went into the kitchen and got two big bowls of ice cream. Then we sat down at the kitchen table. It was dark outside and I had the feeling that Mum and I were the only two people in the world who were awake. Everything was so still and quiet. Everything except the kitchen clock. Tick. Tick. Tick.

Had it always been that loud? There was something about the sound that depressed me. I didn't know why. It had something to do with Alice but I couldn't make the connection.

When Mum started talking, it made me jump. She laughed and so did I. The sound of her voice made me feel a lot better. "Lily, I want you to know that I understand how hard all this is on you. It may seem like it's impossible to get my attention these days, but I will always make time for you if you need me. If there's anything on your mind, or if you have any questions about Alice, you can talk to me."

"It's OK, Mum," I said. "I'm doing fine. Really."

What I didn't tell her was that I didn't need to ask any questions. I had my own source of information at Hope House – namely Susannah.

★

"Please play cards with me. Pleeaeeease." Susannah was hanging on to my arm and trying to get me to play with her.

"Later," I promised. "Let me go and see Alice first and then I'll play cards with you. I promise. Why don't you go find Rusty and see if he'll play with you for a little while?"

"Rusty's not here. His old girlfriend is in town and he went to have lunch with her. He hopes that she's breaking up with her new boyfriend because he's a bum," she added.

"Did he tell you that?"

She shook her head. "No. But I heard him telling Mrs Brady about it."

Maybe it was because she was so little that people forgot she was around, but she was better than a bugging device. She had the scoop on everything – and everybody. I hoped she'd grow up to be a private detective, since it would be a shame to let all that natural snooping ability go to waste.

For instance, Susannah had all the dope on the Graham–Ambrose romance. Susannah knew that Dr William Graham had taken Dr Emily Ambrose out for dinner and it had been a very romantic evening.

Dr Graham is a psychologist and the head of Hope House. His wife died about ten years ago of leukemia. For the last several months, he's been dating Dr Ambrose, this really beautiful resident at Hope House.

Susannah overheard Dr Graham making restaurant reservations for two at the most expensive and elegant restaurant in Somerset. He gave them very detailed instructions about what table he wanted and what kind of flowers to put on the table. Susannah and I thought he might be planning to propose. But it turns out it was just a birthday celebration.

Susannah was also pretty savvy about who was friends with who. It didn't surprise me to find out that Alice had become a popular resident at Hope House. That's just Alice. Even ill and bald and wearing pyjamas, she still had that spark that got people excited. Seems the other kids were in the habit of gathering in Alice's room before lights out.

Since I usually left in the early evening, I was never around for these get-togethers. It made me a little depressed to hear about them. I couldn't help feeling left out.

It also made me sad that it was Susannah who told me about them, and not Alice.

Susannah tugged on my arm again. "Will you bring your pom poms sometime and let me play with them?" she asked, changing the subject as she followed me to the lift. "I want to be a cheerleader when I grow up," she said. "And I want to be popular. And I want to have lots of friends. And get good marks. And be just like you," she finished with a grin.

I started laughing. "What makes you think I'm popular and have lots of friends and get good marks?"

"Because Alice says so. She talks about you all the time. Last night I was in her room until Rusty made me go to bed. Alice told us about your date with Jason and all the great stuff that goes on at your school." She sighed. "I wish I could go to school with you."

Boy! Everybody was enthused about school except for me. If only Alice knew how disconnected from school I really felt. If only she knew that without her, nothing seemed real. Nothing had any meaning. I couldn't tune in.

- I went to my classes. I had conversations with people. I even smiled and waved at some of them in the hall. But I was just going through the motions. Sleepwalking through my days. I didn't feel alive and awake until I got to Hope House and saw Alice.

★

Both Brenda and Alice perked up when I walked in. It made me feel good knowing they looked forward to my visits.

Then I noticed that there were two other girls in the room. Both of them were teenagers, and Alice introduced them as Linda and Marie.

"What's new?" Alice asked me.

"Not much. What's new round here?"

"Who cares?" Linda giggled. "It's not like there's a whole lot to report round here."

That wasn't the way I heard it from Susannah, but I let it pass.

"Who is Somerset playing next week?" Marie wanted to know.

I had to think a minute. There were banners all over the school. Hmmm. Oh yeah. "Plainsville," I answered.

"My cousin's old boyfriend goes to Plainsville," Linda squeaked. "He's really nice. Are there any nice guys at Somerset?"

I shrugged. "I suppose so."

"Like who?" Marie asked.

"Oh, I don't know. Just different guys. I still don't know very many people's names."

"Haven't you done *anything* exciting lately?" Alice pressed.

The blank look on my face must have answered

the question, because Brenda's face fell and Alice began to blush. Brenda shot Alice a strange look and then lowered her eyes. All of sudden, I got the message. I was embarrassing Alice. She was *ashamed* of me.

Who could blame her? According to Susannah, she'd been bragging about me all over Hope House. And now, instead of breezing in like a big wheel – I was plopping myself down like a big dud and expecting four sick kids to entertain me. I started blushing, too. *I* was ashamed of me.

Alice threw me this look, like she was pleading with me to come through for her. I knew she was counting on me and I made up my mind not to let her down.

"Well," I added, "unless you count sneaking out last night."

Alice's eyes got as round as saucers. "What!" she shrieked.

Four pairs of eyes were glued to me and I got this rush of adrenalin.

"It's Mum," I sighed. "She's got the idea that since Jason is fifteen, he's too old for me to date. So I had to sneak out to see him."

"Oh, Lily!" Alice squealed. "When did this all start?"

"Well, I didn't want to talk about it because it's

been a secret from Mum. But Jason and I have been sitting together every day during lunch. Hey, all the other cheerleaders have boyfriends and dates. Shouldn't I?"

"Absolutely," Alice said solemnly. "You go for it, Lily. Now tell us about last night."

All four girls leant forward like I was about to start handing out the secrets of the universe.

And that was the beginning of my career as a compulsive liar. I don't know what came over me. Once I got started, I couldn't stop.

Maybe it was because I was the centre of attention. Usually, I was content to let Alice take the spotlight. I'd never wanted it before. But now . . . well . . . what can I say? They were so obviously impressed with me it was irresistible. And they really wanted these tales from the outside world. They needed them. So I started making up all kinds of stuff that wasn't true.

I told them that Captain Connie was my best friend at school. I told them that I'd been asked to join a whole bunch of clubs at school. And I told them that Jason was madly in love with me and that we were the Romeo and Juliet of Somerset High.

I was really pouring it on thick. After a while, I began to worry that maybe I was making a mistake.

But when I saw the look on Alice's face, it convinced me that I was doing the right thing. She hadn't looked as happy and excited since the day we'd joined the cheerleading squad.

It's pretty crazy when you think about it. And I suppose it was because Alice and I were so close. But more than anything else, I wanted her life, and she wanted mine.

8

There are a lot of good reasons not to lie. Offhand, I can't tell you what they are. All I can tell you is that it wasn't long before my lies backfired on me.

Every day I went to Hope House and gave them an update on my fabulous school career. But as well received as my stories were, I began to get the impression that Alice didn't really want me there. I'd show up and she'd look surprised and say something like, "What are you doing here?"

One day she blew up. "WHY ARE YOU HERE?" she yelled. "It's Tuesday. Didn't you tell me that the squad was getting together at the diner this afternoon to celebrate Stacy's birthday?"

She threw a pillow at me and grinned to show me she wasn't really angry. "Get out of here. Just because I'm ill is no reason to let me ruin your social life."

"You're not," I insisted. "Believe me. I'd rather be here with you and Brenda than at a cheerleading get-together."

"Well, I wouldn't," she said. "Really! I appreciate you coming to visit me, but I'd rather have you go out and do all the fun things I wish I could do. That way I at least get to hear about them. So go! They're probably waiting for you."

"Go!" Brenda echoed, throwing her own pillow at me.

What could I do? I left. I said goodbye and walked out to go to a totally fictitious party.

I stood out in the hall at a complete loss. What now? I couldn't be with Alice and Brenda. And I didn't want to go home.

Talk about ironic. I'd started this whole thing so that Alice would want me around. And it had produced the exact opposite effect.

I was almost out of the front door when I remembered Susannah. I found her in the ground floor lounge. When I walked in, she looked up and pouted. "I hate being the littlest one here," she said. "Nobody wants me around – not even you. You're just like Janet's brother. Whenever there's somebody older to hang out with, you play with them and not me."

I understood how she felt. Alice didn't want *me* around either. It wasn't for the same reason, but it didn't make it hurt any less.

The other thing that hurt was realizing what a small, selfish person I was.

If our positions were reversed, I'd want Alice with me every minute no matter what. I wouldn't care if she had a cheerleading meeting or a boyfriend or a party. I'd expect her to stay with me. Because being together would be the most important thing in the world to me. So why didn't she feel the same way?

The answer was pretty obvious. I wasn't as important to her as I used to be. She had new friends now. Brenda. The other kids. The staff.

I pulled Susannah into my lap and hugged her. "I want you around," I said. "I'll be your friend."

"Promise," she pleaded. "Promise you won't ignore me when there's older kids around?"

"I promise," I said. "Twin's honour."

"Twin's honour? What's that?"

"That's what Alice and I used to say when we promised each other something. We said 'twins honour' because that was the most important thing we could think of to swear on."

Susannah settled back into my lap and thought about that one for a while. "I wish I had a twin,'" she said. "And I wish her name was Lily." Then she gave me a sly smile. "If I had a twin, she'd read me stories."

"OK, OK," I laughed. "You've got me where you want me. What's it going to be?"

She jumped off my lap and ran to the book-shelf. Then she came running back with a whole armful of picture books and dumped them on my lap.

I could see we were going to be there a while. Oh, well. It wasn't like I had anything better to do – no matter what Alice and Brenda thought.

That was how my double life started. Every afternoon, I'd stop on the ground-floor sitting room and hang out with Susannah for an hour or two. "Hide out" would be more accurate.

The ground-floor sitting room was hardly ever occupied. Very few people came in there during the afternoon. Everyone knew I played with Susannah sometimes, but nobody had any idea how much time we spent together and how often I was there in the early afternoon.

I didn't worry too much about Susannah spilling

the beans. She was a little chatterbox, and everybody but me had a tendency to listen to her with only one ear.

After I read to Susannah, I'd go to Alice's room and say I'd been at a cheerleading meeting. Or a yearbook committee meeting. Or a party planning meeting.

Alice and Brenda ate it up. Every once in a while, Brenda would look at Alice and say something like, "Next year you and I can work on the yearbook". Or "Next year, maybe you and I can double date".

I'd be sitting there thinking, *oh yeah!* It just killed me imagining Brenda and Alice doing all the things together that Alice and I had planned to do. Taking the school by storm. Walking down the hall arm in arm. Going to parties together. I wasn't going to let it happen.

I'd had a plan up my sleeve for a while. So far, it was going pretty well. But I didn't tell Alice. Or Mum. Or *anybody*. They wouldn't have approved.

"I'm tired of these stories," Susannah whined.

She must not have been feeling well that afternoon because she'd been cranky and whiny ever since I'd arrived.

"Do you want me to take you to your room?"
I asked. "Maybe you'd like to lie down for a
while."

She shook her head and looked sad. "No."

"Want to watch television?"

"No."

"Want to play cards?"

Long sigh.

"Well, what do you want to do, Susannah?"

"I want to go to the park and ride my bicycle
and do all the things I used to do before I
came here."

Poor little kid. It broke my heart. The next
thing I knew, she was crying. "Don't cry," I
begged her. "Please don't cry. Let's read a story."
I held up her favourite book. I'd read it to her
fifteen times at least. She never got tired of
it.

But she just buried her face in my shoulder.
"I'm sick of hearing stories about other kids doing
things. It just makes me feel worse."

"Then I'll tell you a story about you," I said,
getting this great idea.

That got her attention. "Me?"

"Yeah. I'll tell you a story about you." I was
really sweating this. But I thought maybe it was
time to use my imagination for something besides

lying. "Once upon a time, there was a little girl named Susannah. And —"

Before I could say another word, she interrupted me. "Is this a pretend story? Because if it's a pretend story, I want to pretend I have a twin — just like you."

"OK!" I agreed. I proceeded to make up a story about two twins named Susannah and Lily. I didn't have to make up too much. It was a true story about me and Alice when we were little.

From that day on, all Susannah wanted was twin stories. She never got tired of hearing them.

I never got tired of telling them either.

9

"Lily!" I stopped when I heard somebody calling my name. I turned and saw Captain Connie and Tony waving me over.

I walked to their table to see what they wanted – even though I already knew. I'd hardly talked to them in weeks. I hadn't gone to any games. I hadn't been to any meetings. And I never went to the cafeteria any more. It was too hard to sit there surrounded by all those people who were laughing and talking. My stomach was usually too knotted up to eat anyway. The only place I felt relaxed enough to eat was at home or at Hope House with Alice.

I usually spent my lunch period in the library pretending to study. But I wasn't. I was just killing time. In fact, every minute I wasn't at Hope House with Alice, I was just killing time.

"Hi," I said.

"Listen, Lily," Connie said. "Whatever you want to do is fine with us, but you haven't shown up for any games or meetings."

"Sorry," I said in this sort of sarcastic voice. "I guess I've had more important things on my mind."

"We understand," Tony said in this dizzy voice that was beginning to get on my nerves. "My sister had appendicitis last year and everybody in the family got . . ."

I glared at her and she trailed off. I didn't care if her sister had appendicitis last year. It wasn't the same thing at all. If she'd had any brains she would have known that.

"We're not criticizing you," Connie said. "We understand you're going through a tough time. I'm just trying to determine whether or not you want me to include you in the schedule."

I didn't say anything, and she sighed. "It might be fun for you." She sounded like somebody coaxing a little kid. "There's a game this weekend. If you want to come out with us, Tony and I could get together with you after school and bring you up to speed."

I shook my head. "I think you should replace

me. I'm pretty busy these days."

Connie and Tony looked at each other as if to say, *we tried*. "OK then," Connie said. She pulled out a little notebook and wrote something in it. "I'm going to notify the faculty advisers that you're going inactive for a while. But let's not make it an official resignation. That way you can leave your options open. If you want to reactivate at any point, all you have to do is let me know. OK?"

"Fine," I muttered.

"How is Alice doing?" she asked as she scribbled in her notebook.

"She's lots better," I answered, even though I wasn't sure that was true. Alice felt pretty bad a lot of the time. But then, everybody said that was a normal reaction to radiation.

"We were thinking of visiting her," Tony said. "If you think she's up to it."

"No!" I said quickly. That was the last thing I wanted. If they came and visited Alice, Alice would find out what a bunch of lies I'd been handing her. "She's better, but she's still too sick for visitors."

"That's too bad. We'll hold off then." Connie shut her notebook with a snap. "But tell her we're thinking about her. And tell her we'll hold her spot on the squad until she's well enough to come back. Yours too," she added.

I knew she was trying to be nice. I knew she was doing her best to act like a friend. And I knew I should say thanks. But I couldn't bring myself to do it. I didn't want their friendship – or their sympathy. So I didn't say anything at all. I just watched her walk away. Captain Connie. Head cheerleader. Major big cheese. My "best friend".

I forgot about Tony until I felt her tap me on the arm. "What?" I barked.

She looked startled, but she held her ground. "I just wanted to tell you that you might want to think about working on the yearbook. It's not as demanding as the squad." She seemed to be choosing her words very carefully. She dropped her voice until it was almost a whisper – as if we were conspiring behind Connie's back. "It's a different bunch of kids. Sometimes the whole cheerleader scene can be overwhelming. But the yearbook staff is different. More low key. If you feel like it, just come by and meet some of the kids. You don't have to do anything. You can just watch if you want."

Talk about bizarre. In the totally phoney life I told Alice about, I was *already* big buddies with the yearbook staff. And now here was Tony offering me a chance to make it true.

But I didn't take it. I just mumbled something about seeing her later and hurried away.

On my way back to class, I passed Jason. This was really not my day. But I suppose after all the times he'd tried to talk to me and I'd brushed him off, he'd finally given up. Because this time he walked past me and looked in the other direction.

It was almost Thanksgiving and I was looking forward to having four days to spend with Alice.

On the Monday afternoon of that week, I stopped by the ground-floor sitting room and told Susannah a couple of twin stories, as usual. Then I headed upstairs to see Alice.

I could hear her and Brenda before I was even halfway down the hall. They were laughing and singing and I could see Alison standing in the doorway laughing with them.

"What's going on?" I asked, coming up to join them.

Alison pointed inside the room and grinned. I had this big smile on my face too. When I looked in the room, it was all I could do to keep smiling. What I really wanted to do was scream and break things.

If you can believe it, Alice and Brenda were sitting up in their beds wearing identical wigs – really smart ones, although they were too old for them.

"What do you think?" Alice grinned. "Somebody donated a whole box of wigs this week."

Brenda looked in a mirror and pouted. "I vant to be alone," she said in a deep voice with a foreign accent. I think she was supposed to be Greta Garbo.

Alice began to laugh hysterically, like it was the funniest thing she'd ever heard in her life. "I vant to be alone, too," she mimicked. "Vot about you?" she said to me.

I am alone, I thought. I'd never felt so lonely in my life.

Alison clapped her hands. "I've got a brilliant idea. You know they're planning a costume party for the night before Thanksgiving?"

"Another one?" Brenda said. "We've just had one for Hallowe'en."

"Dr Harding says costume parties are good for everybody's morale – including his." Alison laughed. "He says he gets tired of looking at people in pyjamas and white coats."

"You had a Hallowe'en party?" I choked out. This was the first I'd heard about it.

"Yeah," Alice said. "But it didn't start until about eight o'clock and you'd already gone home."

"It was really fun," Brenda said. "The volunteers made everybody masks out of paper sacks. We had a ball."

Every year, Hallowe'en had been a special night for me and Alice. We loved thinking up costumes that involved both of us. In the past, we'd been Raggedy Ann and Raggedy Andy, Tweedle Dum and Tweedle Dee, and Mickey Mouse and Minnie Mouse. When Hallowe'en had come along this year, I didn't say anything about it because Alice hadn't been feeling well. She hadn't said one word about it either. I'd assumed it was because she wasn't interested.

On Hallowe'en night, I'd stayed home by myself watching horror movies and thinking about Alice. I couldn't believe Alice had been here partying with Brenda. To top it off, she hadn't even told me about it.

"If I can dig up a couple of matching sequinned dresses, will you two come as two of the Supremes?" Alison asked.

Alice and Brenda squealed.

"That would be so cool," Brenda said.

Alice grabbed a banana from her bedside table and began to sing into it. "Baby. Baby. Baby. Ohhhhhh. Yeahhhh." Then she tossed the banana to Brenda, who caught it with no trouble at all and sang the same thing only an octave higher "Baby. Baby. Baby. Ohhhh. Yeahhhh."

They leaned across the space between the beds and high-fived each other.

"Are we a team? Or are we a team?" Alice crowed.

Rusty and Dr Gordon had come along and they stood behind Alison watching the fun.

"You're great," Rusty grinned. "You'll be the hit of the party."

"We'll see you there," Alice shouted as they all drifted away from the door. Then she turned towards Brenda. "Unless we're otherwise engaged in throwing up," she added in an undervoice.

Brenda rolled her eyes. "Tell me about it."

The whole time, I'd been standing on the sidelines watching. Before I knew it, great big tears were rolling down my cheeks.

Alice jumped out of bed and ran over to me. "What's wrong, Lily? What is it?"

All I could do was shake my head. How could I possibly say it? It would sound so childish and so selfish. How could I say to her, *you didn't invite me*

*to your Hallowe'en party. You didn't even say anything
to me about Hallowe'en. And now here you are, all
excited about dressing up with Brenda.*

Nope. I couldn't say that. So what did I do? I
told another great big lie. "It's Jason," I sobbed.
"We had a fight."

"Ohhhhhh," they both said, really interested
now.

"That's right," I sniffed. "We were supposed
to go to a party the night before Thanksgiving.
I told Mum I was going to a party with Connie.
But I was really going with Jason. Now we're not
speaking to each other and the date's off."

"That's terrible," Brenda said, giving me a
sympathetic look.

I peeped through my fingers to get Alice's
reaction. Her face wasn't sympathetic. It was
disappointed – like it was *her* date that had fallen
through.

"You and Jason have broken up?" she repeated
in this quiet voice.

I nodded, feeling relieved. Now I could at least
stop making up stuff about me and Jason.

"You'll get back together," Alice said, all of a
sudden sounding really confident and enthused.

"No we won't," I snivelled.

"Yes you will," she insisted. Her voice was so

urgent and upset, it made me see how important all my lies had become to her. Somehow, her identity was all tied up with mine. She wanted a boyfriend. She wanted to be popular. She wanted to be a cheerleader. Since she couldn't do all those things, I had to do them for her.

"Of course you'll get back together," Brenda said. "But probably not this week. So you'll just have to plan on partying with us sick kids that night."

It was what I'd been waiting to hear. But I didn't want to seem too eager. I wanted the invitation to come from Alice.

What did I hear from Alice's side of the room? Nothing.

"There were a whole bunch of these wigs," Brenda went on. "We'll get a third one and ask Alison to get us as third dress. That way we really will be the Supremes."

I peeped again at Alice, still waiting for her to put her two cents in. Something along the lines of *Please, Lily. It won't be any fun unless you come*, would have been nice.

The silence was deafening. Alice climbed back on to her bed looking vaguely depressed.

"It'll be great. Won't it, Alice?" Brenda prompted.

"Yeah. Sure," Alice said.

It didn't sound too convincing.

"So will you come?" Brenda urged. "Please say you will."

This was the best I was going to get. So I took it.

"Sure," I said. But I was really peeved that it was Brenda begging me to come and not Alice.

10

The night of the party rolled round and Mum and I both went to Hope House at about six o'clock. There was a reception and support group meeting for parents in the downstairs sitting room.

As soon as we got there, Mum ran into a couple of the other mothers she had met over the last few weeks. They headed for the coffee pot and I made a beeline for Alice's room.

She and Brenda were already wearing their wigs. They were also wearing the most outrageous sequinned dresses I'd ever seen. A third wig and dress were laid out for me at the foot of Alice's bed.

When Alice looked up and saw me at the door, her face fell. "It's you," she said.

"You were expecting maybe Tom Cruise?"

She smiled. "No. I just hoped that you might have made up with Jason and gone to the other party."

"Are you kidding? And miss this?" I laughed and held up the dress. It was only about five inches too long. "Perfect fit."

Brenda stood up and I saw that hers was too long, too. "Alison said she'll come by and pin them up for us. She's also got some old tapes that she's been trying to talk us into miming to."

Alice rolled her eyes. "How corny," she muttered.

"Are you OK?" I asked her. It wasn't like Alice to shirk the spotlight.

"Sure," she said shortly. Then she grinned. "Get dressed and let's get ready to party." Her eyes had a little sparkle and I felt better. For a minute, she sounded like her old self.

The party was a real eye-opener. Since I mostly saw Alice in her room, I hadn't met too many of the other kids. I also hadn't realized what a mover and shaker Alice was around Hope House.

It had taken Alison a long time to get all three dresses pinned up. So the party had been going for a while before we walked in.

We stood in the door for a few minutes watching

the crowd. There were about eighteen teenage kids who looked like patients. Some were residents of Hope House, some were outpatients, and some had come over from St Stephen's. There were another five kids who looked like they were friends or family. Then there was Rusty and Alison. Dr Steve wasn't there, which was disappointing, but Dr Harding was. He had on a hilarious "rap" costume and he stood by the stereo ready to play DJ.

Rusty spotted us first. "Alice!" he called out.

Alice. It was like some kind of magic word. A signal. A cue that the fun was about to start.

The whole room looked towards her and every face lit up. The party was really a party now.

It was like standing in the wings watching a great actress getting ready to make her entrance. These kids needed her. They needed her joy and her enthusiasm. She knew it and she wasn't going to let them down.

Alice stood up straighter and broke into a big smile. She bopped right into that room like she owned the place. "Crank it up," she called to Dr Harding, twitching her shoulders to the music. "What's with this place?" she demanded. "How come I don't see anybody dancing?"

"We don't have enough guys," shouted a girl who was hooked up to a rolling IV.

113

"Oh yeah?" Alice laughed.

In a burst of inspiration she found a paper plate and a magic marker. Everybody crowded round her to see what she was up to. She took the paper plate and drew eyes, a nose, a mouth and a moustache on it. Then she attached the plate to a hook on the rolling IV and twisted a paper napkin into a bow tie.

Presto! The rolling IV became Fred Astaire. Everybody laughed and applauded as the girl twirled around the room, dancing a waltz with her IV.

"Make one for me," shouted a boy who also had a rolling IV.

Alice drew another face – female. Then she took two more paper plates and strategically placed them on his IV like a bra.

"Madonna!" they all screamed.

It took Alice about thirty seconds to get that crowd going. It was amazing. Don't ask me how she did it because I don't know. All I can tell you is that suddenly, the whole room was jumping.

There were some great costumes there. Some kids were dressed like rock stars. And some kids were dressed like monsters. Some kids just had on a bunch of goofy clothes. But whatever they had on, they all looked wonderful.

"Wanna dance?" a boy dressed like Frankenstein asked me.

"Sure!" I pulled my wig on tighter and we started to boogie.

"My name's Ed," he said with a smile. "Are you an inmate or a visitor?"

"I'm Alice's sister. We're twins," I added in case he hadn't noticed.

"Oh, right! You must be Lily. You're like a *legend* around Hope House. Our ambassador to the outside world."

Some ambassador. I was having more fun at the Hope House party than I'd had the whole school year. I felt connected in a way that I never did at school. It was because I was where I belonged – with Alice.

Ed and I talked for a while and danced to another couple of songs. Then I heard somebody shout "FLOOR SHOW!"

Brenda came over and began pulling on my dress. "It's show time," she laughed.

We got up and mimed to some Supremes songs and I had a ball. The extrovert in me finally came out of the cupboard. Even after Brenda and Alice had pooped out, I was still up on the stage lip-miming away to one of Diana Ross's greatest hits.

I threw back my head and opened my mouth as

wide as possible trying to match up with the last note. When I tipped my head all the way back – the wig fell off.

The audience roared and I made a big show of looking embarrassed and trying to put the wig back on. I put it on backwards, and then sideways, and then backwards again.

Finally I stepped down and Rusty came over and gave me a big bear hug. "You're great!" he laughed. "I see where Alice gets all her personality."

He had it backwards. But heck, who was I to argue with a genuine registered nurse?

Out of the corner of my eye, I could see Alice slipping quietly out of the room.

"Thanks," I said. "Listen, I, ummm, have to go to the bathroom. Will you excuse me?" Then I hurried after Alice.

She was already at the lifts when I got into the hall. "Wait," I shouted. I ran over to her and when I got up close, I could see that her face was green. "What's wrong?"

"I don't feel well all of a sudden," she said. "But you don't need to leave. Stay here and have a good time."

"Don't be ridiculous," I argued. "Let's go back to your room."

We barely made it back in time. As soon as we hit the door, Alice ran for the bathroom and threw up for a while.

She came back out and flopped on the bed. "You know what," she sighed, pulling the wig off and dropping it on the floor.

"What?"

"Cancer stinks," she said.

I sat down in the chair next to her bed and reached for her hand. "It won't last for ever, Alice. You'll be out of here in a few months. I was talking to that guy, Ed. He said he's going home next month."

"Yeah," she said in this flat voice. "Right."

Before either one of us could say anything else, the door opened. Susannah came in, wearing her nightgown and holding a teddy bear.

"You didn't come and visit me tonight," she said accusingly.

"I'm sorry. But tonight was a party."

"For the big kids?" she asked.

"That's right. For the big kids."

She looked at me for a long time. "You promised you wouldn't ignore me just because there were big kids around."

She was right. I had broken my promise. "What can I do to make it up to you?"

Susannah climbed up in my lap and settled in. "Tell me a twin story. Tell me the story about the time the twins found the lost dog."

"Again?"

"Again," she nodded.

I began to tell her a story about the time Alice and I found a lost dog. We walked all over the neighbourhood ringing door bells, trying to find out where the dog lived. After two hours, we found the right house. But by then, we'd wandered so far away from our own house, that *we* were lost. We were little kids and we couldn't remember our phone number. So the people who owned the dog had to walk *us* over the neighbourhood, ringing door bells and trying to find out who we belonged to.

Alice began to laugh. "I'd almost forgotten that," she said. "Remember Mum's friend who worked for the newspaper? She wrote a funny story about it and there was a picture of us and the dog in the newspaper. We have lots of copies of that newspaper. I wonder where they are."

"In Mum's big box of photographs," I answered. "I saw them not too long ago."

"Will you bring me a picture?" Susannah begged. "Please. I want to see what the twins and the dog looked like."

"They looked like us," Alice said. "Only smaller." She smiled. "Tell her the story about the time we were going to run away from home." She chuckled. "By the time we packed two of everything the suitcase was too heavy to carry."

"Oh, right," I said. Then I started to laugh. I'd almost forgotten that story. It all came back as I told it to Susannah.

Alice got ready for bed as I talked. She put on her nightgown and washed her face and got into bed, adding little bits and pieces of the story. Things that she remembered that I had forgotten. Like how we decided to take a lot of stuff out of the suitcase, but couldn't agree on what to leave behind. Finally, it was so late and so dark, that we decided to run away from home the next day. By then, of course, we'd forgotten why we were running away so we called the whole thing off.

Alice turned out the overhead lights and got under the covers. The only light in the room was the wedge of light under the bathroom door and the big beam of moonlight that came streaming through the window. It was so cosy, I wished we could sit there all night.

I wasn't the only one who felt that way. Alice let out a long contented sigh and so did Susannah. "Tell her the story about the time we tried to find the pot of gold at the end of a rainbow," she suggested.

Both Alice and Susannah fell asleep to the sound of my voice. By the time I'd finished that story, Susannah's head was heavy against my arm.

I looked at my watch. It was getting late. Mum was probably waiting downstairs for me.

Very quietly, I began to tiptoe out with Susannah in my arms. I'd drop her off in her own room on the way out.

Before I reached the door, I heard Alice's voice. "Good night, Lily."

"I thought you were asleep," I whispered.

Her voice was low and drowsy. "Almost," she said. "Thanks for coming tonight. I know it must have been a pretty big bore for you."

"Are you kidding?" I said. "I had a ball."

"I'm sorry," she whispered.

"What are you sorry about? I told you, I had a great time."

"I'm just sorry I'm ill. This wasn't what I had planned for this year. I'm sorry you get stuck hanging around here because of me. I think I'm trying to say I'm sorry I let you down."

I went back over and sat down. "Come on, Alice. Lighten up. You're not letting me down.

You can't help it that you're ill. Didn't you read that little pamphlet they gave us?"

I was teasing her now. We'd been given pamphlets about the kinds of emotions people have when they get cancer. It explained that cancer just happens – you don't get it because you deserve it, or you get bad marks at school, or you were careless.

She smiled sleepily. "I know. I'm just feeling sorry for myself. I guess because we're twins, that means I'm feeling sorry for you too. I'm too tired to make sense." She closed her eyes and began to mutter – almost to herself, "I don't really need to feel sorry for you, do I? Things at school are going great."

"Right," I said. "Couldn't be better."

She opened one eye and it gleamed in the moonlight. "And I'm sure you'll make up with Jason."

"Absolutely," I agreed. "All he has to do is send me a thousand roses and bring me the golden fleece."

She laughed and turned over, pulling the covers up closer. "Good night," she said. "And thanks again. For everything."

11

By Christmas, Alice was through with radiation and had started on chemo. It was rough stuff. She was so sick they sent her back to St Stephen's for a few days while they experimented with different anti-nausea drugs.

That's where she was on Christmas Day. She felt so rotten that Mum and I had to open her presents for her. We had a lot of things for her – books, games, lacy pillows, and a whole collection of scarves in every colour.

The hospital had all sorts of Christmas activities going on. But Alice was too ill to take part and Mum and I were too depressed.

Needless to say, Alice wasn't the least bit interested in food. So in the late afternoon, Mum and I went to a restaurant near the hospital that advertised a complete Christmas dinner.

The seating hostess showed us to a nice table by the fireplace and we sat down. I looked all round, trying to work out who the other people were. Did they all have family members in the hospital?

"This is nice," Mum said, looking round too. She fiddled with the holly and berry arrangement in the middle of the table. "It's almost full in here," she said. "I wonder who all these people are?"

"I was trying to work that out, too," I said. Just then I spotted somebody. "Look." I hissed. "It's Dr Graham and Dr Ambrose. Over there. Over your left shoulder . . . don't be obvious."

Mum glanced over her shoulder, pretending to look for a waitress. "You're right," she said. "Is there something going on between them?"

"Oh boy, is there! It's better than a soap opera." I told her about their budding romance, passing along all the details I'd heard over the last few weeks from Susannah and Alice and Brenda.

"Sounds like you're really wired in to what's happening at Hope House," Mum said with a laugh. She looked at me for a few moments, and her face turned serious. "Are you as wired in at school?"

I could feel myself getting tense. I'd had a feeling Mum was going to get around to this conversation at some point. Her life had been so busy since Alice had been diagnosed. Too busy to monitor my activities. Between work, and visiting Hope House and consulting with all of Alice's doctors, she hadn't had much time for me at all.

Whenever she'd asked me about cheerleading and school activities, I'd given her vague answers. She'd seemed satisfied and that was fine with me. Parental scrutiny would have been counter-productive to my plans at that point.

"Well?" she asked. "How are things at school?"

"OK," I said.

She stared at me a long time. Then she took a sip of her water. "Twin's honour?" she asked.

I blushed, thinking about the report card that was stashed beneath my underwear at home. "Twin's honour," I answered, crossing my fingers under the table.

The you-know-what hit the fan a few days after school started back in January. Alice was back at Hope House. The anti-nausea drugs were fairly effective so she was coping better with the chemo.

I'd been in her room visiting her. Mum was supposed to be working late that day so I'd planned on taking the bus home. I was on my way out the front door when I heard somebody call my name.

It was Andrea Shepherd, the social worker who lives at Hope House. Mum had talked to her several times, but so far I'd managed to avoid her. She seemed too much like a grown-up version of Alison to me.

She was standing at the door of her office and beckoning to me. "Could you step in here?"

Like it or not, we were going to have a talk.

Guess who else was sitting in her office?

Mum. That's who. She held a piece of paper in her hand and tapped it against her knee. My face turned beetroot red. I knew what that piece of paper was.

Andrea has one of those low, soothing voices that "helping professionals" always seem to have. "Lily, do you think the three of us could have a talk?" Putting it to me like I had a choice, you see. What rubbish! I had no choice and all three of us knew it.

I sneaked a look at Mum's face. Hard to read. She'd obviously been briefed ahead of time. Told to stay neutral and not get excited.

Andrea shut the door and motioned to me to sit down. I took a chair and the three of us sat facing each other round a low glass table.

Mum held up the piece of paper. "The school

125

called me this afternoon," she said. "I sent a messenger from the office over to pick up this."

She handed me a xerox copy of my report card. Three Ds and a C.

"I want you both to understand something," Andrea said smoothly. "This is not at all unusual under the circumstances. When a sibling is ill, very often the other sibling begins to act out anger and frustration. Sometimes that acting out takes the form of misbehaviour. Sometimes the marks suffer. What we need to talk about is how we can help Lily express those feelings in a more constructive way."

Mum's lip began to tremble. She was really upset. "I think I have to take responsibility for this," she said. "Lily, darling, I'm sorry. I'm so sorry. I know that between work and Alice, I haven't had much time for you. I'm going to try to correct that. I give you my word."

It was awful. Here was Mum thinking it was all her fault. Promising to do better when she was already doing the very best she could for everybody. I couldn't let her take the blame. I might have been a liar, but even I wasn't that low.

"It's not your fault," I argued. "This isn't some stupid way of getting your attention. I promise."

"Then what is it?" Mum asked. "These marks

are so unlike you. You've always been an excellent student."

Andrea turned to me. "Lily, everybody here at Hope House is aware of how attentive you've been to your sister. We all admire you enormously for that. But maybe you're spending too much time here and not allowing yourself enough time to study. Perhaps we need to restrict your visits until you get caught up."

"NO!" I shouted.

Both of them jumped.

"Please don't keep me from coming here," I begged.

"But if you can't keep up with your school work . . ."

"I can," I said. "I can keep up. I have plenty of time to study."

"Then what is it?" Andrea asked.

"I just didn't do the work," I said.

"Why not? Is it too difficult?"

"No. The work's not too difficult."

"Then why have you done so poorly?"

I hung my head.

"Lily," Mum urged. "Please, darling. Help us to understand."

"I wanted to fail," I whispered. "So I'd have to repeat my first year."

Andrea sat forward. "Why?" she asked.

I didn't want to cry but I couldn't help it. I could see all my plans coming apart. All my dreams disappearing. "So that Alice and I could have our first year together. Do all the things we talked about doing. I want us to go through school together. I want us to go to college together. If I don't stay behind now, I'll lose Alice for ever," I sobbed. "Nothing will ever be the same. Nothing! Ever!"

I heard a sob from the other side of the table and saw Mum frantically reaching for the box of tissue. "Oh, Lily," she choked. "Oh, Lily!" She got up and stumbled out of the door.

I started to follow her but Andrea put her hand on my arm and kept me in my seat. She handed me some tissues and let me cry for a little while.

Finally she started talking. She told me how it was important to live for today and how stupid it was to sabotage myself. Would Alice want me to fail? Would Alice want me to repeat a year of school for her sake?

"No," I sobbed. "She wouldn't. That's exactly what's bothering me."

"What do you mean?" Andrea asked gently.

"*I'm* worried about being separated but *she* doesn't seem to care. Being twins isn't as important to her as it used to be. If it were, she'd be worrying about being a year behind me, too."

"Your sister is ill, Lily. She has a lot on her mind. One thing that's on her mind is the fear that she's holding you back."

I shook my head. No matter what she said, it didn't explain Alice's attitude. It had become painfully obvious that I wanted to be with her more than she wanted to be with me. Why? Why didn't Alice want to be with me any more?

"Your sister loves you, Lily. She talks about you all the time. You are important to her. Being twins is important to her. I know that. Everybody here does. She talks about how popular you are. How involved you are in your school activities. How clever you are." She gave me a wry smile. "You are clever – in spite of that report card."

Andrea thought she was making me feel better, but she was making me feel worse. All the things that Alice was so busy bragging on me about were big fat lies. I wasn't popular. I didn't have any friends. I wasn't involved in any activities.

"Talk to Alice about your feelings," Andrea suggested. "If you feel like your twinness is slipping away from you, share those fears with her. The best thing you can do is be honest with her."

I blew my nose and nodded. Andrea was right. It was time to be honest with Alice – about everything. I hated being a liar. I promised Andrea I'd talk to Alice the next day.

It took me three days to get up the nerve to confess. I got to Hope House a little earlier than usual. Susannah was in the hall and she let out a happy shout. "YOU'RE HERE!"

I picked her up and swung her around. "Well, of course I'm here. Aren't I usually here?"

"The last time they had a party you didn't come in the afternoon. You just came for the party."

"What are you talking about?" I asked.

"There's a big party tonight. It's Alison's birthday and everybody's invited – even me. Didn't you know? They've been planning it for two weeks!"

"No," I said. "I didn't know about it. It's just for the patients, huh?"

She shook her head. "Nope. It's for everybody. Even me."

I wished she'd stop saying that. Obviously, it wasn't for everybody. Alice hadn't said a word to me about it. Neither had Brenda. There was a conspiracy going on here.

Just then, Mrs Brady swept by me carrying a

huge plate of cookies. Rusty trailed behind her with a cake.

"Hi, Lily," Rusty said. "Staying for the big party tonight?"

"I'm not sure," I said in a tight voice.

I put Susannah down and pushed the button to call the lift.

"Aren't you going to tell me a story?"

"Later," I promised. "I need to go and see my sister first."

The lift took for ever to come, so I ran up the stairs, getting angrier as I went. What was wrong with Alice, anyway? Why didn't she want me at Alison's birthday party? Why hadn't she wanted me at the Thanksgiving party?

What nerve! Here I was ready to put my whole life on hold for Alice – and she didn't even want me around.

All the way up to the second floor, I fumed. I stormed into the hall. We were going to have this thing out once and for all.

But just before I got to her room, the door swung open and out walked a bunch of girls. I was so surprised it took me a moment to realize who they were: Connie, Tony, Stacy, and practically the rest of the cheerleading squad.

"Bye, Alice," Connie said. "It was great to see

you. Sorry we didn't come sooner, but Lily told us you weren't up to visitors."

I ducked into the broom cupboard and waited until they'd all filed out and gone down in the lift.

When I thought it was safe, I came creeping out and went to Alice's room. Alice was sitting up in bed. When she saw me, her eyes narrowed.

Brenda looked back and forth between me and Alice. "I'm getting out of here," she said in a scared voice. Then she hurried out of the door.

Alice glared at me. "I can't believe it. I just can't believe it. You told them not to come and see me! All this time I thought nobody cared. Why did you do that?"

I glared right back. "I suppose for the same reason you didn't tell me about Alison's party tonight. I don't notice you trying to include me with *your* friends. Why should I make an effort to include you with *my* friends?"

"They're not your friends," she hissed at me. "Why are you such a liar? They showed me pictures from the games and the parties. You know what? You weren't in one single picture. They told me they've hardly seen you since I got ill. You've been lying to me. Lying about *everything*. Why? Why did you lie to me?"

"Because you *made me lie to you!*" I burst out. "You didn't want to hear the truth."

"THAT'S NOT TRUE!" she yelled.

"IT IS TRUE!" I bellowed. I was really furious now. It hadn't occurred to me until we started yelling how angry I was. "You made it clear that you didn't want to hear about my life unless I was a big social success. I had to be Miss Popularity – so YOU could feel like Miss Popularity too. You were just living through me. Using me so you could feel good about yourself. You don't care about *me* any more. Or about us. Or about staying friends. Or being twins. Or *anything*! You didn't want me here at your party on Thanksgiving. And you don't want me here tonight."

Alice drummed her fists against her blanket. "Why would you even *want* to be here?" she demanded. "That's what I don't understand. It's so pathetic. Why would you want to be around a bunch of sick kids when you could be doing things with Connie and Tony? What's wrong with you, anyway?" Her lip curled into a sneer. "Can't you find anything better to do than mope around here mooching brownie points? Racking up gold stars for being so nice to poor little Alice and Brenda. Please. Give us a break, will you? One Alison around the place is plenty."

133

She was white and shaking and so was I.

"Fine," I spat. "I do have better things to do. Lots of better things to do."

"Name one," she challenged – just as nasty as she could be.

I didn't bother to answer. I wasn't going to give her the satisfaction. Instead, I turned round and stormed out.

Mum came out of the kitchen when she heard me slam the front door – hard.

"What's the matter?" she asked when she saw my face. "What's wrong?"

"Nothing!" I shouted. "Except that I hate Alice. I hate her guts. I'm never going back to Hope House. Alice can spend the rest of her life there as far as I'm concerned because I DON'T CARE IF I NEVER SEE HER AGAIN!"

12

Looking back, there are so many things I wish I'd done differently. And there are lots of things I wish I hadn't said. It still just makes me ill when I remember saying that to Mum. It must have been so painful for her.

You see, she already knew that Alice was probably going to die. She'd known it when we were sitting in Andrea's office, too. That's why she'd been so upset.

The worst part is, she knew it the whole time I was being stubborn and obnoxious and refusing to go back to Hope House. She tried to get me to change my mind and visit. But I wouldn't. I wouldn't ask about Alice, either.

If I had, she would have told me the truth. But I didn't ask. I didn't want to know.

It must have been hard on her, having to keep that knowledge to herself. But I see now that she couldn't tell me the truth until I was ready to accept it.

Every time Mum asked me if I wanted to go to Hope House, I said I was busy. Actually, it was true.

I was being tutored in the library every afternoon so that I could get caught up. Mum, Andrea, and the school had all ganged up on me and convinced me that I needed to do something about my marks. I didn't give them an argument. What was the point in failing now? Alice had made it pretty clear that she didn't care whether we went through school together.

Some of my teachers volunteered to help me. They all knew that my sister had cancer so they were very understanding.

Sometimes they recruited other kids to work with me. Imagine my surprise when one day my Spanish teacher started apologizing all over the place because she had a teachers' meeting. Not to worry, she told me. One of her older pupils had agreed to work with me.

Guess which one?

That's right. Señor Jason.

When he sat down next to me in the library I

thought I'd shrivel up and die of embarrassment. He had to think I was the biggest weirdo in the world. A mere five months ago, we been kissing on my front porch and after that I'd acted like I didn't know him from Adam.

"Hi," he said with a smile. "Remember me?"

No. Never seen you before in my life. What was your name again? I forced myself to smile back. "Let's see. The guy from the party. Right?" *Perfect. Friendly with just a pinch of sarcasm.*

"*Sí*," he chuckled. "Since you haven't spoken to me in months, I thought maybe you'd been hit on the head and got amnesia. Or else that I'd offended you."

Even though I didn't feel like talking about it, I knew I owed him an explanation. "I don't know if you heard this," I began, "but . . ."

"I know," he said quickly. "Your sister's been ill. I'm sure it's been rough. You don't need to apologize. How's she doing, anyway?"

Luckily, I didn't have to answer. Tony appeared behind Jason and gave us both a big dizzy hello. It was almost like a reunion, and I wondered if they'd planned it.

"What are you two doing?" she whispered.

"Getting ready to study irregular verbs," Jason whispered back.

Tony giggled. "Can I talk you into looking at these first?" She pulled out some proofs of the yearbook pages.

"Wow," he said. "These look great. What do you think, Lily?" He passed them over to me.

Beside every picture of a graduating senior was his or her primary-school picture. They'd asked every senior to list the top ten things they'd learnt since the first picture was taken. Some of the lists were funny, and some were serious. Either way, it gave you some insight into each personality.

"This is great," I said. "Whose idea was this?"

"Mine," Tony giggled. "I'm glad you approve." She grinned at me. "Come with Jason to the next yearbook committee meeting if you want. We can always use more help."

"Thanks," I responded. "Maybe I will."

She stood up and stuffed the pages in her bag. "Tell Alice hello."

Tell Alice hello.

How? We weren't speaking.

Mum was visiting Hope House every day. But I was too hurt and too angry. Most of all, I was too ashamed. Alice had struck a nerve. She'd been right about a lot of things. What I had done *was* pathetic – hiding out at Hope House so I wouldn't have to make friends on my own. Letting people think I was there because my sister needed me, when it was the other way round.

I wasn't like Alison. I was worse. At least Alison went to Hope House to give. I had gone to Hope House to take. To lean on kids who were sick for emotional support.

It was embarrassing.

Then one day, Susannah called me. I suppose she got my number from somebody on the staff. She wanted me to come and visit her.

"Pleassee," she wheedled. "Pleeease come. Come and tell me a twin story. There's nobody my age here again. The big kids won't play with me."

Under the circumstances, it seemed like a legitimate reason to go. Susannah really did need me.

"OK," I laughed. "OK. I'll be there tomorrow," I promised. "Meet me in the ground-floor sitting room."

"Lily!" she shouted. There was no doubt that Susannah was glad to see me. She threw herself into my arms. I was glad to see her too, and I hugged her as hard as I could without squishing her.

"I've been waiting for you," she complained. "Where have you been? You're late."

"I had to meet some friends after school," I said.

"Older kids?" she asked.

"Yeah. But I didn't just ignore you because there were older kids around. I was working on a school activity."

For once, it was true. I'd finally let Jason and Tony talk me into proofing copy for some ads one afternoon and I'd got the bug. Tony had been right. The yearbook was fun and the staff was more low key than the cheerleading squad. You could hang around the yearbook room and talk or not talk. It was a comfortable place for me.

My marks still weren't good enough to make me eligible for the yearbook committee – but let's just say the faculty saw their way towards letting me participate in an unofficial capacity.

Just then, Rusty came barrelling into the lounge carrying a big tray with afternoon snacks on it. When he saw me, he was so surprised he nearly dropped the tray.

Susannah and I sprang forward in time to prevent a major catastrophe.

"Lily!" he cried. "I knew you'd come." He stuck his head out of the door. "Lily's here," he shouted.

Pretty soon, I was surrounded by Dr Ambrose and Dr Rhodes and a couple of kids I'd talked to in the halls. Even Alison came rushing in with her guitar.

I had worried that it might be awkward seeing all those people. I'd been afraid they would think I was an awful person and give me the cold shoulder. But they didn't. They were all hugging me and telling me how great it was to see me.

There was something slightly hysterical about it – they were *too* happy to see me. It was Alison who finally spilled the beans.

"It's really great that you came to see Alice. She needs you now more than ever."

The way she said it made me nervous. "Why? What's going on? What are you talking about?"

There was this long silence and everybody looked uncomfortable.

"Didn't you know?" Alison frowned.

"Know what?"

Andrea Shepherd appeared at my elbow. Somebody must have gone to get her. "Brenda died, Lily."

"What!"

"She died last week."

"No."

"We assumed that was why you were here. I had hoped that Alice might have called you."

"Why didn't Mum tell me?" I gasped.

Andrea shook her head. "Alice asked her not to. I suppose she thought it would upset you."

Upset me. That had to be the biggest understatement of the year.

"I'd better go and see Alice," I said quietly.

When I opened the door, Alice was sitting up in bed looking at a magazine. She looked awful. Her face was round and puffy and her eyes were red and swollen. I didn't know if it was from medication or from crying.

She didn't say anything when she saw me but she closed the magazine.

Both of us looked towards the other bed, which was neatly made up. Then we looked away, not knowing what to say.

"I'm sorry," I said finally. "I'm sorry about everything. I'm sorry I lied. I'm sorry I was cross. Most of all, I'm sorry about Brenda."

"I'm sorry, too," she choked. Then she was crying – big tears rolled down her swollen cheeks. "I'm so sorry. I'm so sorry. I'm so sorry." She repeated it over and over, sobbing into her hands.

I rushed over to her, trying hard not to cry

myself. "Cut it out, Alice. You don't need to be sorry. You were right – about everything. I'm the one who should be sorry. And I am."

She shook her head and just kept crying. "I'm sorry. I'm sorry. I'm sorry," she chanted. She couldn't stop so I put my arms round her we rocked back and forth. "Don't cry," I whispered. "Please. Brenda wouldn't want you to cry. You know she wouldn't."

"I'm not crying for Brenda," she managed to sob. "I'm crying for you."

For me!

"What are you going to do, Lily? *What* are you going to *do*?" she gasped.

I didn't understand what she was saying at all. "What do you mean, Alice?"

"It's awful to lose the one person who understands. The one person you can share everything with. It's so lonely."

"But that should be *me*," I protested. "I know you were close to Brenda. But can't you try to be close to me again? I used to be the person you shared everything with. Why did you stop? Please don't stop."

"I don't want to share my life with you any more. Don't you get it?" she sobbed. "I've got nothing to share with you but pain and fear and

being sad. That's why I didn't want you here."
She took a deep shuddery breath. "I wasn't trying
to exclude you. It was the only way I knew to
get you to hang around school – make friends, do
things with other people. But you were right," she
sniffed, "I did put too much pressure on you. It was
because I needed to know you could make friends
without me. Not depend on me to be happy."

She sat back and cleared her throat. "You can't
depend on me any more, Lily."

Alice stared at me for a long time, like she was
trying to make up her mind whether or not to tell
me something. She put her hand on top of mine.
I looked down at her hand and saw how small and
frail it had become.

"You can't depend on me any more because I'm
going to die," she said quietly.

The minute she said it, I realized I'd known it for
a long time. I'd just been pushing the thought as far
away as possible. Never letting the idea really take
hold. Because life without Alice would be . . .

Never mind. I can't even begin to write about
my feelings. There aren't any words to describe
those feelings.

I threw my arms round Alice and held on for
dear life. If I could just hang on tight enough,
she wouldn't die. She *couldn't* die. She was my

sister. My twin. My best friend in the whole world.

But I couldn't hang on that tight. Nobody could. We both knew it. "I'm sorry," she sobbed again into my shoulder. "I'm so sorry."

I don't even remember leaving Hope House that afternoon. All I remember is walking for hours and hours. Eventually, I wound up sitting on a bench across the street from the burger joint. The same place Alice and I had sat before school started. It looked just the same. There were cars circling the block and lots of kids going in and out as if they didn't have a care in the world.

It occurred to me that I ought to resent them. But somehow, I didn't. They had a right to their lives. They had a right to laugh and flirt and be silly. They had a right to grow up.

And so did I.

It all became clear to me then. There was only one thing I could do now for Alice. And that was let go. Get on with my life and let her get on with what was left of hers. She was feeling responsible for me. She always had. It was time to let her off the hook.

The next day, I hurried to Hope House the minute

145

school was over. Alice's door was closed but I didn't knock. I pushed the door open and walked in – just as if it were the room we used to share at home.

She had been crying again. I could tell from the way her eyes looked. There were also about a thousand used tissues lying on the floor. It made me want to cry too, but I didn't.

"OK," I said swallowing hard. "OK. I understand now. I really do. You don't need to worry about me. What you did was right. It worked. I am spending more time at school. I am making friends. Believe it or not, I spend some of my afternoons with Tony and Jason."

Alice looked sceptical. She sat back and blew her nose. "Please," she said, sounding more like her old self.

"No fooling," I said. "I really do. I'm helping them with the yearbook. We go over the ads and the copy and then we go out for a soda."

"Really?"

"Really."

"So?"

"So what?"

"So tell me about Jason. Is he still interested? Do you think he likes you? Do you like him?"

Then we both started laughing. Alice hadn't

146

changed a bit. I rushed over to the bed and she put her arms round me. We sat there for a long time, not saying anything but holding each other.

"What about the squad?" she asked finally.

I shook my head. "I don't think so."

"Lily!" she protested. "If I promise not to be afraid of dying, will you promise not to be afraid of Connie?"

"It's got nothing to do with being afraid of Connie," I insisted. "And I'm not afraid to do it by myself either. I'd rather spend time on the yearbook, that's all."

She looked disappointed.

"I'm beginning to realize cheerleading was always more important to you than it was to me," I explained.

She furrowed her brow in confusion. "I don't understand. If you really didn't want to do it, why did you let me talk you into it?"

"I went along with it because it was something we could do together – something to share. That's all."

The door opened and Susannah came creeping in. "You're supposed to be visiting me," she pouted.

Alice began to laugh and so did I.

"See," she said. "You're popular whether you like it or not."

Susannah climbed up on the bed with us. "What are you talking about?"

Alice and I looked at each other. How did you tell a five-year-old you were talking about death? And then I realized we weren't talking about death. We were talking about life – and making the most of it.

"What have you got there?" Alice asked her. Susannah was clutching something in her hand – it was dirty and crumpled, but when she handed it to Alice, Alice recognized it and smiled. "It's us. It's the picture of us with the lost dog."

"You gave it to me a long time ago," Susannah said, taking it back and smoothing it against her leg. "Will you bring me another picture sometime? This one is all crinkled."

That gave me an idea for something that Alice and I could do together that would be meaningful for us both. The one thing the two of us would always share was the past. We'd shared that past with Susannah and it had meant a lot to her. Maybe it could mean something to other kids, too.

13

I was afraid Mum might be upset. She'd spent hours putting those photo albums together. Then I came along and wanted to take them apart.

As always, Mum was a sport. She let me take all the pictures that I wanted.

You see, I needed them for the book that Alice and I decided to write. We found all the pictures that had a funny story connected with them. Then we took turns writing about the story. One chapter from my point of view. And one chapter from Alice's.

It was an entertaining book and it was amazing how much stuff it made us remember. Like the time we had new neighbours with a little boy our age. On the day he moved in, Alice ran over and introduced herself as the fastest kid in the world.

To prove it, she challenged him to a race – her on foot, him on his bicycle.

He took off pedalling and disappeared around the block. Of course, *I* was waiting at the finish line.

That story still cracks me up when I think about it. I'll never forget the expression on the kid's face when he saw me standing there tapping my foot. I asked him what took him so long and he nearly fell off his bicycle. There's a picture of all three of us shaking hands and laughing about it afterwards.

There were a lot of pictures and a lot of stories. I was almost afraid we wouldn't finish in time. We did, though, and we couldn't have done it without Tony. She was the one who scurried round and found people to donate money for the printing and the photographic reproductions. She designed the cover and the page layouts too. Tony was a real friend to us both during those last few weeks. So was Jason.

Jason got the book printed by the same people who print the school yearbook. I don't know how he did it, but he got them to finish it practically overnight.

Twin's Honour is on sale now in the gift shop at St Stephen's hospital. The proceeds all go to Hope House and the book is "dedicated to Susannah,

Tony, and Jason, without whose help this book would not have been possible".

On the last page, there's a picture of me and Alice sitting on her bed at Hope House. She has a scarf over her head and her face is swollen from the steroids. But everybody who sees it says we still look like twins. No matter how many nice things they say about the book, the thing that makes me happiest is to hear that we still looked like twins.

Alice died in late May, just before school broke up for the summer. I wasn't there, but Mum was. She told me that it had been very peaceful and that Alice hadn't been in any pain.

On the day of Alice's memorial service, I went to my morning classes. Alice had made me promise that I would. She was afraid that if I didn't go, the school might not respect her instructions.

She'd been adamant about not wanting the traditional moment of silence. What Alice wanted was a non-traditional moment of noise – and she got it.

There was a morning assembly in Alice's honour. Connie led the squad up on the stage. When they gave the signal, every single pupil stood up and gave one long, loud, raucous cry of joy.

It was great. You should have heard it. Actually, maybe you did. It was loud enough to raise the roof.

And maybe somehow, somewhere, Alice heard it too. I hope so. She would have got a big kick out of it.

Freshman Heartbreak

The girls of **Freshman Dorm** are back in **Freshman Heartbreak,** the fifteenth book in the new series about three best friends and their freshman year at college.

If Josh knew about **Winnie**'s fling, he'd flip out! But he doesn't have to find out, does he?

When **KC** swears nothing will keep her from following Peter to Europe, is she inviting disaster?

Lauren's still hoping for a reunion with Dash – then she sees him with another girl ...

Liza seems determined to break every rule; roommate Faith has had enough. This is *war*!

Price £3.50

Also available:

No. 9 Freshman Schemes
No. 10 Freshman Changes
No. 11 Freshman Fling
No. 12 Freshman Rivals
No. 13 Freshman Flames
No. 14 Freshman Choices
No. 16 Freshman Feud

All at £3.50

Anastasia's Chosen Career

Anastasia had visions of what the modelling studio would look like. There would be a tasteful bronze sign attached to the wall beside the front door. Inside, there would be soft carpeting, with some colourful cushions strewn on the soft couches in the waiting room. The lights would be bright, and there would be a gorgeous receptionst in designer clothes at a big semi-circular desk.

Anastasia glanced up at the dark staircase. Somehow this place seemed different: she wasn't sure it could look like a modelling school if it spent the next fifty years trying. Perhaps she'd better go home after all . . .

£3.50

ORDER FORM

To order direct from the publishers just tick the titles you want and fill in the form below:

Name _____

Address _____

_____

_____

Send to:
Department 6, HarperCollins Publishers Ltd,
Westerhill Road, Bishopbriggs, Glasgow G64 2QT

Please enclose a cheque or postal order to the value of the cover price plus:

UK & BFPO: Add £1.00 for the first book, and 25p per copy for each additional book ordered.

Overseas and Eire: Add £2.95 service charge. Books will be sent by surface mail but quotes for airmail despatch will be given on request.

A 24 hour telephone ordering service is available to Visa and Access card holders: 041-772 2281